Shaking
The
THE NOVEL

HS Press

The Shaking
THE NOVEL

EL CANTARE

Ryuho Okawa

HS PRESS

Copyright © 2022 by Ryuho Okawa
English translation © Happy Science 2025
Original title: *Shousetsu Yuragi*
HS Press is an imprint of IRH Press Co., Ltd.
Tokyo

All rights reserved. Without limiting the rights under copyright reserved above, no part of this publication may be reproduced, stored in, or introduced into a retrieval system, or transmitted, in any form, or by any means (electronic, mechanical, photocopying, recording, or otherwise) without the prior written permission of both the copyright owner and the above publisher of this book.

ISBN13: 978-4-8233-0451-4

First Edition

All images © Shutterstock.com, used under license.

Contents

The Novel The Shaking 8

Afterword 155

Major cities and parks in the novel

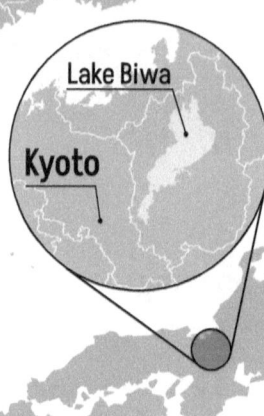

CHINA
NORTH KOREA
SOUTH KOREA
Lake Biwa
Kyoto
JAPAN
Tokyo

✹ MAIN CHARACTERS ✹

Yuho Oyama .... Grand Master of the Sun Church
Shohei Reiwa .... Principal of Happy Christ School

THE UMA RESEARCH CLUB MEMBERS

Hideo Yamakawa .... kendo club
Hikaru Daichi .... karate club
Jiro Kawabe .... boxing club
Setsuko Minami .... biology club
Emi Natsume .... science club

Tosuke Ishikura .... freelance journalist

Zempukuji Park

Kichijoji

Shinjuku

Tokyo Skytree

Tokyo

Shibuya Tokyo Tower

Tokyo Bay

Enlarged map of Tokyo

Inokashira Park

1.

It begins again.

It always starts at 3:00 a.m.

Sometimes, I feel like I am not myself. Perhaps, I'm dreaming. Anything is possible in a dream, for dreams are rich in creativity.

It usually starts with a light shaking. My legs start twitching, then, my right or left arm that is stretched out of the blanket. Sometimes, my fingers start closing and opening on their own.

My wife is asleep in the bed to my left. She usually takes a mild sleeping pill, so she doesn't wake up unless I scream. Unlike the Chinese proverb that says, "Sleeping in the same bed but having different dreams," we sleep in separate beds and always have different dreams.

Before going to sleep, I read through today's report for the second time, as I usually do.

What caught my attention was the two-page article in a magazine called *Western Economy*.

A freelance journalist named Tosuke Ishikura, a drop-out of Aomori University Faculty of Letters, had written some criticisms about the school where I am the principal. This is his way of making a living. I now think that it was a mistake to have invited such a rotten guy on a bus tour to our school. It was like letting loose a wolf into a flock of sheep. I was too soft to give this "wolf" a free lunch and to show him around my school.

After falling asleep with such thoughts, *it* started at a little past 3:00 a.m.

As I dream, I leave my physical body with a little "shaking." At such times, I must be a soul, itself. I cannot see myself nor see myself reflected in the mirror, but I still feel like I have a head, hands, legs, and torso.

Tosuke is jealous of me because I graduated from the renowned Kaisei High School and then the University of Tokyo with a degree in Education. That guy tries to hide his ugly, jealous feelings by shooting down people he envies in the name of social justice.

The Constitution of Japan guarantees freedoms of expression, speech, and the press, but this doesn't mean that it explicitly allows "freedom of jealousy." Whether an opinion is an expression of mere jealousy or fair criticism should be judged by sound public opinion, and an evil one must be eradicated.

My newly established Christian school, in particular, is protected under freedom of religion as stated in the Constitution, so bad-mouthing it—even on the pretext of "freedom of expression"—must be condemned accordingly. Our school is connected to the Lord God through Jesus Christ and upholds *noblesse oblige* as its motto. So we need to be especially cautious against the "werewolves" that are prejudiced against religion and say, "Those who believe in religion are idiots" or "Religious leaders make money under the name of religion."

They often try to defile sound and faithful students and drive them to lose their faith.

My transparent body flies over Tokyo in the middle of the night.

Inside an old apartment by the river, I see Tosuke. He's still typing away on his old laptop at this ungodly hour. It's obvious that he's living the life of a night owl. Freelance writers who libel others as a way to blackmail them are exploited by publishers as disposable workers. As such, they tend to live their day-to-day life as sloppily as cockroaches.

Behind Tosuke is a woman from a hostess bar who often comes to stay in his apartment. She is sleeping on a mattress that reeks of ammonia. Many empty beer cans are scattered around her pillow, one of which stands upright to put her cigarette butts in.

I—the soul of Shohei Reiwa—enter Tosuke's two-bedroom apartment and read the article he is working on. He is writing about a political scandal under a different name again. He is using false information that says a politician received three million yen from a particular religious group. He knows that even such disinformation can get a politician sacked if other media follow up on it. And if he succeeds in doing so, his name will become well-known and he'll be reputed as "The Slasher" among journalists.

Fear is most effective when it creeps in slowly.

So first, I, who have become a spirit body, sneak into the dream of Tosuke's mistress. In her dream, she is attacked by about 10 rats that come out of the holes in the four corners of the room. She lets out a loud shriek.

Without looking back, Tosuke hisses, "Shut up!"

Next, I make the fluorescent lamp on the front left corner of Tosuke's table flicker.

"Damn it! It was just getting exciting." As he swears, he places an emergency flashlight on the windowsill. His computer screen is bright enough for him to keep typing.

The mere story of a politician receiving three million yen is not enough to make the article interesting, so he adds a fake story of how the politician ended up caught in a honey trap set up by a Chinese spy at a Chinese restaurant.

I—the soul of Shohei Reiwa—believe that fabricating a story should not be forgiven even if writing critical articles on politicians can sometimes benefit the public.

I collect the moisture from around the room and drop it on Tosuke's head like raindrops.

Tosuke turns around and yells at the woman, "You bitch! How dare you splash the rest of the beer on me!"

The woman wakes up and says, "Baby, I was just having a dream about a snake being devoured by 10 rats. I hope you're not writing an article that would put your life in danger."

"If this article is that risky, they should be paying me at least 100 million yen for the manuscript." Tosuke curses Kancho-sha, the publishing company that commissioned this job.

All this was part of Shohei Reiwa's experiment; he started to examine how much he could do in the state of astral travel.

Maybe I could be like Batman, he thought to himself. He began to see its potential.

A Christian school principal by day, and "Batman" by night.

"Yeah, that could be pretty interesting." He returned to his sleeping body around 4:30 a.m. that morning.

2.

Soon it was dawn.

Principal Shohei Reiwa's house stood on the premises of his Academy. Although one could call it an "official residence," it was more appropriate to call it a "house" because it was merely a three-bedroom home.

The principal's wife's name was Mitsuko. It was his second marriage. After his former wife, Shoko, left with their two children, he chose to marry Mitsuko who belonged to the same Christian group. Shohei's ex-wife was a career woman, and they started disputing after Shohei joined the Christian organization called "Sun Church." When Shohei became a staff member of Sun Church and his income fell significantly below hers, she left him without hesitation. Indeed, it was a rational decision.

Shohei chose faith over money. Oh, how pleased God must have been with him. Eventually, Shohei and Mitsuko were blessed with two children, who now attended a nearby elementary school.

The establishment of the Academy, which Shohei was entrusted with, was of course sponsored by Sun Church. Shohei was chosen as the first principal because of his excellent academic records: a graduate of Kaisei Junior and Senior High School and the University of Tokyo Faculty of Education.

The official name of the Academy was "Happy Christ School" and it was often abbreviated as "HCS." It aimed to produce well-rounded students who are good in both studies and sports without the need for a prep school. Shohei, himself, was good at kendo (Japanese fencing using a wooden sword); he used to belong to the kendo club during his Kaisei days.

Shohei was especially proud of the environment where the Academy was located. It stood on a hill in front of Inokashira Park, and the students could enjoy the beautiful scenery of the four seasons of Japan. The magnificently large pond spread beyond the windows of the second-floor classrooms, making it seem as if they were at an "ocean front" or had an "ocean view." Because the park was famous for its cherry blossoms, they could also enjoy the pink flowers in spring. The cherry blossoms could even be seen from the principal's house. Ever since he was assigned to be the principal of this combined middle school and high school five years ago, he produced excellent students who passed the exams to enter top-flight universities such as the University of Tokyo, Waseda University, and Keio University almost every year. There was even a year when the Academy was ranked among the top ten schools in Japan with the highest percentage of students accepted to Waseda University. About 40% of the students entered the Academy from the beginning of high school.

It was this morning when a commotion broke out during the staff meeting. Looking pale, Vice Principal Tatsue Kawaguchi brought an enlarged photo to the principal. It was a photo taken at night. It showed a room at the corner of the school building but with a green-bodied creature that resembled a *kappa* (a water imp) with black, almond-shaped eyes. What is more, the creature was looking out of the window from the inside. It would have made more sense if it were the other way around and the creature was peeking into the room from the bushes outside. It would be less strange if a suspicious person were peeking into the school building from the outside. Or if a *kappa* happened to be in a photo of the pond in Inokashira Park, they couldn't rule out the possibility of a legendary creature living there. However, it should not have been possible for such a creature to be *inside* the music room located on the second floor of a building that was securely locked at night. This was a serious matter that jeopardized the fundamental safety of the students. The school not only had day students from neighboring cities but also many boarding students; 70% of the students were from distant areas and lived in the boys' dormitories and girls' dormitories adjoining the school.

The teachers passed the photo around and they all started speculating: "Is this a *kappa*?" "No, it looks exactly like a Grey alien," "Could it just be a prank?"

Principal Shohei Reiwa also studied the photo carefully. He then remarked, "There's no way our students would make such a picture as a prank. A *kappa* would have hair and a plate on its head, but this one doesn't. So this small green creature is most probably an ET. It's possible for a UFO to land in Inokashira Park at night and secretly release a probing Grey."

In any case, if any students were harmed, the school would lose its reputation and many prospective students. So the principal directed the staff to increase the number of surveillance cameras and night lights. He also ordered Vice Principal Tatsue Kawaguchi, who resembles the actress Keiko Kitagawa, to gather the students who know about the photo in a separate room and hold a ritual ceremony to perform "Prayer to Exorcise Evil Aliens"—a prayer granted by the Grand Master of Sun Church.

Tatsue was a certified Japanese teacher and a nun from Sun Church, so she was quite experienced in conducting rituals.

After school that day, she gathered the students who knew about the photo and a few teachers to hold a ritual ceremony in that particular music room. Tatsue led the prayer. She rang the bell on the staff of *kerykeion* (caduceus) and performed a group ritual prayer ceremony to repel malicious aliens. When she then performed an exorcism on each student, Principal Reiwa witnessed Tatsue's knees trembling during the ceremony.

Tatsue was one of the best female priests in Sun Church who had undergone spiritual training for 30 years. The legs of such a long-serving priest were trembling so violently that she was about to float into the air.

This isn't good, thought the principal. He decided that this situation required the Grand Master's judgment. He felt that he, too, needed to investigate what was going on as early as tonight.

The principal told the group that he would consult with the Lord and dismissed the gathering for the time being. Tatsue was trembling terribly; this was no ordinary opponent. When the principal asked Grand Master Yuho Oyama in the Head Cathedral, he received a reply saying, "It must be an alien cyborg—a Grey."

That night, too, the principal was "shaken" at 3:00 a.m. His soul went up through the roof of his house, flew over to Inokashira Park, and circled around it at about 100 feet in the air.

After a while, he saw an unidentified, bright-gold object descending from the sky. The object wasn't so big. It was a small UFO of about 33 feet in diameter. It stopped about three feet above the water at the center of the pond, and out came two golden Greys with black, almond-shaped eyes. It was as if they were walking on an invisible sidewalk. When they came to the shore, Principal Reiwa in the form of a soul called to them, "What on earth do you want with our school?"

The Greys took out some small robots that were shaped like beetles and stag beetles from the pouches on their stomachs and said, "We've heard that an interesting school was built, so we are carrying out an investigation. Don't worry, we won't hurt you."

The principal gave them a firm warning, saying, "Make sure to put the safety of our students first."

3.

It was the next day. The mystery was identified spiritually, but its existence had yet to be proven in a tangible way.

If the students were harmed or abducted, it would become a police matter, but at this moment, there was no point in filing a police report. And it was out of the question to consult the Japan Self-Defense Forces and tell them, "A UFO descended on Inokashira Park last night, so please do something about it."

The Japanese mass media could not be trusted, either. It would only lead to freelance journalist Tosuke Ishikura bad-mouthing the Academy.

The principal and vice principal discussed the matter, and decided, for now, to collect photos and video footage that would serve as evidence. After that, it would be better to consult with the board of directors of Sun Church and the Faculty of Future

Industry of Happy Christ University (HCU), the affiliated university of Sun Church.

Principal Reiwa and his staff chose five students from the eleventh grade to conduct the research. They chose eleventh graders because twelfth graders had university entrance exams to study for and because if they chose middle schoolers, it would worry the parents.

The five members formed the "UMA Research Club (UMA meaning Unidentified Mysterious Animal, or Monster)." The research entailed potential danger, so three male students were recruited from the kendo club, karate club, and boxing club. They were accompanied by two bright female students from the biology club and science club.

Hideo Yamakawa from the kendo club proudly said he could knock the Greys out with his wooden sword. Hikaru Daichi from the karate club was full of drive and said, "I wanna land a spinning kick on the back of the Grey's head!" Jiro Kawabe from the boxing club was beaming with confidence and said, "One uppercut is all I need to beat it." Setsuko Minami from the biology club said, "I'd love to capture it alive, put it in Ueno Zoo, and give the panda bears a run for their money." She, herself, resembled a panda. Emi Natsume from the science club said, "My family runs a photo studio, so please count on me when it comes to videos and photos."

How positive these students were. For them, their curiosity was stronger than their fear.

Two teachers were chosen to supervise the UMA Research Club: Mr. Ishiwatari, a fifth-degree holder in kendo, and Ms. Yamaoka, an avid researcher of ancient creatures.

Under the pretext of bird-watching, the UMA Research Club started their activities by setting up surveillance cameras on the path that the aliens would have to take to get from Inokashira Park to the Academy. They also positioned a high-end camera on the roof of the Academy to record images of UFOs flying above Inokashira Park. It was set up to automatically capture any moving objects at night.

It was unlikely for any utility helicopters from the Japan Self-Defense Forces or civil helicopters to fly below an altitude of 65-100 feet from the pond's surface. They just needed to clearly distinguish UFOs from birds.

And so, the second night arrived.

Something similar to a flash of lightning struck the surface of the pond three times.

The lightning was captured on camera, as well. But there weren't any images of UFOs. Only couples in the night, homeless people, and stray cats and dogs were recorded on the video cameras set up in the large trees.

They weren't able to find out the truth behind the whole series of events.

So on another night, the group set up a green tent in the park. They were trying to determine what the lightning was at the very least.

Around 1:30 a.m., the first lightning struck the pond. The water in the pond glowed dimly and bubbled like a hot spring.

The second lightning hit at a little past 3:00 a.m. When the lightning struck, it seemed as though a golden cross appeared on the surface of the pond.

The third lightning hit around 4:30 a.m. This time, something quite different happened. Water spewed out of the pond, like a fountain, and occasionally emitted a bright light. They could see a UFO-like object floating, but it was not showing up on the camera due to its translucent nature.

Setsuko from the biology club said, "Maybe the UFO is sucking up the water and carp from the pond."

Jiro from the boxing club blurted out softly. "Darn it. Let me give 'em a punch."

Emi from the science club remarked, "That lightning must be transmitting an underwater probe. It's possible that the aliens have constructed a secret base at the bottom of Inokashira Pond. Perhaps they're storing their UFO there during the night. They can't possibly be flying the UFO all day long. They, too, need to get some rest."

The following day, the members of the UMA Research Club rowed a boat to the center of the pond and investigated the area. But they couldn't find anything out of the ordinary.

However, there was a slightly abnormal reading on the radiation detector they had borrowed from Happy Christ University (HCU).

"What's going on? The pond is only 6-10 feet deep at most!" Hideo, the group leader and a kendo club member, said in a confused voice.

On their way back, Hikaru from the karate club spotted an out-of-season stag beetle resting in the crotch of a cherry blossom tree. He climbed the tree and caught it with his right hand. As he flipped it over and the five of them stared at the belly of the stag beetle, it suddenly exploded with a "POW" and turned into smoke. The stag beetle disappeared from Hikaru's hand.

"That's not fair! They destroyed the evidence!" exclaimed Jiro from the boxing club.

"What on earth are they plotting?" muttered Hideo.

"Maybe they're investigating something before causing serious trouble," speculated Setsuko from the biology club. "I have a hunch that something much more serious is going to emerge very soon."

Serious trouble occurred the following week.

4.

The following Monday morning, the school staff meeting was in uproar. Dozens of investigators in jackets labeled "Metropolitan Police Department" were investigating the sidewalks and bushes in the neighborhood park. Others were on boats, probing the pond bed with long sticks and nets.

The Metropolitan Police Department wouldn't move so quickly to investigate aliens. Could the UMA Research Club have caused some trouble?

Contrary to Principal Reiwa's concern, a voice called out, "Apparently, a high school girl has been killed."

Media reporters started to flock to the neighborhood.

Oh, no. Was one of our girls from the research club attacked while on guard duty last night?

If that were the case, Principal Reiwa would have to resign.

When he was informed that the victim was a student from Nishiogi Girls' School, he gave a sigh of relief even though he knew he shouldn't be relieved. He was well aware that all human life was equal in value, but he still couldn't ignore whether it was his responsibility or not.

Mr. Hara, the P.E. teacher, reported the details as he rushed into the room wheezing.

"Apparently, the police initially thought the female student was assaulted and killed in the night. But then they discovered the bite mark of a ferocious crocodile-like animal on her body found floating face down in the pond. The body appeared to have been severely damaged."

"Why was there a crocodile in the pond?" asked the principal.

"Long ago, the park had a small zoo. They say one of the reptiles could have escaped and grown large. Another possibility, they say, is it's an abandoned pet crocodile that has grown large in the pond."

"In any case, even TV reporters have now gathered here. So please make sure to inform the students not to leave the campus," directed the principal.

The morning staff meeting was a panic.

The principal was holed up in his office, absorbed in a TV talk show.

"This incident could put an unexpected end to the commotion around the UFOs and Greys," mumbled Principal Reiwa. "The aliens will most probably move to a park somewhere deep in the mountains. The Academy may be safe after all."

There was a knock on the door, and Head Teacher Niimi came in.

"Principal, another concern has come up," he said.

Niimi is a couple of years older than the elite Shohei Reiwa and is a former English teacher at a metropolitan high school. His hair is thinning a little and he is known for wearing very strong glasses.

"What is it?" asked the principal.

"According to the zoo and aquarium experts who studied the teeth marks on the body, the culprit is nothing like a crocodile, a shark, a giant snake, or a wild dog. It seems to be an unknown creature. This will soon be reported in the news, as well. If the incident turns out to be a mysterious case, I'm afraid that people will grow increasingly afraid, and our students will be targeted for interviews and investigation."

"Please prepare a manual for dealing with the mass media as quickly as possible and distribute it to the students by the time they go home. Also, make sure all boarding students refrain from going out at night for the time being," the principal told the head teacher.

"Yes, sir. I will get it done as soon as possible," Head Teacher Niimi said.

Once he left the room, Principal Reiwa locked the door and sat down on the couch. Then, he started to pray in a meditative state. He was preparing to conduct a time-back reading he had learned from Grand Master Yuho Oyama.

After about five minutes of meditation, the principal's body started to shake back and forth slightly. He tried to see what happened last night with his spiritual eyes.

Hmm. I knew the Greys weren't capable of such things. The aliens called Reptilians have finally made their appearance. Japanese people are lagging way behind in terms of alien information. Will the truth be revealed now? But Kichijoji is a city of a million residents. This incident could develop into a more serious matter. If, by any chance, real evil aliens started to attack us with offensive UFOs, would it be possible for the police or the Self-Defense Forces to retaliate? Even if they did, they would have no chance to win. Even the U.S. military's cutting-edge jet fighters would be treated like children's toys.

What is it that I can do? What can we do on our own? Can we maintain the happy lives of the million people in Kichijoji while protecting our Academy? In the end, I will have to rely on Grand Master Oyama, but I want to fulfill my mission as the principal. In the meantime, maybe it's a good idea to discuss what we can do with the members of the UMA Research Club in secret. They may have gained some important pictures or footage.

During lunchtime, Principal Reiwa gathered the five high school students and their two supervisors under his authority. He listened to their opinions.

Hideo, the club leader, insisted, "We should definitely examine whether or not the incident is connected to the Greys and UFOs we saw. We need to know their purpose to figure out how to deal with them. The police are too ill-informed to resolve the issue." As expected, he gave a sound opinion as the best male student.

Emi then said, "We'll analyze the footage from the cameras set up on the rooftop and the large trees and see if any images were captured. We'll divide up the work among ourselves. I'm not afraid. Fear arises when we don't know the cause. We set up the cameras most efficiently, so I'm sure they captured some evidence." She, too, was very reliable.

The supervisor Mr. Ishiwatari chimed in. "Maybe this is a chance to change the world and save the people. Reptilians are nothing to me. I'll definitely beat them with a single strike of my wooden sword."

To this, Reiwa gave a word of warning. "You'd better be careful. The aliens may not be as weak as the alien that appears in a Hollywood sci-fi horror movie by an Indian director."

5.

To assure the public, the police delivered an official statement to the press.

"The case of the murdered high school girl which occurred in Inokashira Park was initially suspected as murder by an escaped pet animal, such as a crocodile that grew too big. It was suspected that the victim was attacked inside the pond. But according to the bite mark, we now think that the culprit was a sex offender, and the bite mark was part of a cover-up. We'll strengthen our investigations in the neighborhood and make sure that the suspect is caught. We'll also increase police patrols at night to prevent any recurrences."

A reporter asked a question. "So is it safe to assume that there are no crocodiles in the pond? Can we assume that boating is safe?"

"Until the culprit is arrested, please be cautious about playing alone or going out at night," replied the police spokesman.

Another reporter asked, "Did you find any suspicious facilities or suspicious people in the neighborhood?"

"There is a research center on psychic phenomena called 'M Research Center,' but so far, we haven't found any evidence of animal or human experimentation being conducted there."

Then, Tosuke Ishikura raised a question. "I think HCS Academy is suspicious. Do you think it's possible that the girl from Nishiogi Girls' School was taken to their boys' dormitory to be raped and killed before her body was made to look like she was attacked by an alligator?"

"We hear that the school has a good reputation in the neighborhood. Most students are polite and it's also a religious school. We at the police don't think all religions are evil in nature."

Tosuke persisted. "You're too easy on them. All religions are cults. You should search the school thoroughly for once. You might find some dead bodies buried in their yard."

The police spokesman gave an order. "Please remove him. We'll only take questions from official staff from TV stations, newspapers, and major weekly publications."

A reporter from NHK (public broadcaster) asked, "Just to confirm, you don't think it's necessary to close the park. Is that correct?"

The police spokesman replied, "Now that the cherry blossom season is over, we don't think there'll be a serious problem. We'll continue to make every effort to ensure the safety of the park so citizens can relax."

Principal Reiwa was relieved as he watched the TV program. At the same time, he thought that the UMA Research Club had to be cautious in carrying out its activities.

Meanwhile, the members of the UMA Research Club were in the room next to the music room. It was their research room. They were analyzing the recordings from the cameras they had collected—the male students collected the ones in the park, while the female students collected the one on the roof. The camera set up by the pond showed a crocodile-type creature, which clearly had two legs enabling it to walk upright. It must have been a Reptilian.

In addition, the rooftop camera captured something like a UFO, which appeared to be a cloud at first glance, descending unnaturally to the park pond.

Hikaru from the karate club said, "I knew it was a Reptilian. But the police would say this isn't enough evidence for a murder case."

Setsuko from the biology club commented. "It happened at night and in the dark, so if somebody says it's a person in costume, we couldn't refute it." She then fell deep into thought.

The research club decided to wait a little while before making their next move to avoid unnecessary trouble with the police.

However, another incident happened on Tuesday night of the following week. It was unusually foggy. The thick fog covered the entire pond and even spread to the nearby buildings.

Hideo, the leader of the research group and member of the kendo club, was the first to notice that something was off. "Could this be the mist that comes out of UFOs?" he said.

Hikaru from the karate club felt uneasy and said, "Another murder might occur."

The fog was so thick that the cameras were useless. Jiro from the boxing club brought out the tools he had prepared. It was quite a primitive method, but it should be effective in detecting the initial intruder. The plan was to stretch fishing lines with bells attached to them across the paths through which the intruders would most likely walk to enter the school grounds.

The members of the research group listened carefully for sounds picked up by the handmade "microphone" as they took turns getting sleep.

However, that night ended in disappointment; there was not a single sign of an intruder.

It was between 8 and 9 o'clock in the morning when the incident came to light. The fog had already cleared away.

At Principal Reiwa's house, the family gathered in the dining room to have breakfast. The principal, his wife Mitsuko, and their eldest daughter Miwako (age 11) were eating ham and eggs with toast. But their son Kazuyoshi (age 9) was not up yet.

"Kazuyoshi, get up, or you'll be late!" His mother Mitsuko called him several times, but there was no answer.

His sister Miwako went to peek in his room and found that his bed was empty. The window was open, and the lace curtain was blowing lightly in the breeze. "He's not here!"

The parents came rushing in, only to find the room vacant.

This had never happened before. They sensed that their son had become a victim of a crime.

Mr. Ishiwatari of the UMA Research Club was the first to be informed. The team was summoned.

Emi said, "Oh, no. We didn't expect that the principal's house would be targeted. We didn't set up the fishing lines and bells here."

"This creature must be quite intelligent. I can't believe it didn't fall for our trap on its first attempt," said Setsuko.

"A prehistoric dinosaur would enter from the most accessible point, so this one at least has the intelligence of a thief," added Ms. Yamaoka.

"In any case, it was our mistake not to have set up any cameras or bells at the principal's house," said Hideo.

"Why don't we three guys bike around the park before the police get here," suggested Hikaru.

Hideo, Hikaru, and Jiro biked around Inokashira Park in search of the principal's son, Kazuyoshi, but they couldn't find him.

"This may be their way of declaring war," said Mr. Ishiwatari as he tightened his grip on the wooden sword.

6.

After Kazuyoshi (age 9) went missing from the principal's house, a strange voice began to echo from the closet at night.

"Open it! Open it!" A small shouting voice of either a boy or a girl came from the closet in Kazuyoshi's room or from his sister Miwako's (age 11) room. It sometimes came from the closet in his mother Mitsuko's (age 40) room and occasionally from the one in the principal's (age 55) room.

Just in case Kazuyoshi was kidnapped for ransom, the family set up a call tracer on their main phone; a 30-second conversation would enable them to identify the location of the kidnapper. But in kidnapping cases, unless the child is released within 72 hours, it usually means he or she is already dead.

The five members of the club got together and exchanged their thoughts.

"If he has already been killed and the voice actually belongs to a ghost, we can't save him," said the club leader Hideo.

Emi said, "I wonder if there's such a thing as 'yokai akete' ('Monster Open-it')."

"Is that a kind of monster? A *kappa*, Slender Man, a dwarf, or a hobbit might be considered a monster, but I've never heard of 'yokai akete'," said Setsuko.

"What if we replied 'Close it'?" joked Jiro.

Emi chimed in. "Then, we should also ask, 'Who are *you*?'"

Of course, nobody was in the closet when the family members looked. So they decided to have Hikaru, a karate fighter, and Emi spend the night at the principal's house in case something happened. They intended to record the voice saying "Open it!" and have it voice-printed. Because the principal's daughter Miwako was still an elementary school student, Emi decided to sleep in her room, while

Hikaru, a second-degree black belt holder in karate, slept in Kazuyoshi's room. They made sure that all other members were also alert and ready for an emergency call.

The club leader Hideo thought to himself. *In three days, the police will likely conduct a thorough investigation of our school and drag the pond in the park again. At that time, we'll have to hand over all the information of aliens we've collected.*

Jiro Kawabe was speculating the same thing. *But in that case, we'll also have to protect our school's reputation and Principal Reiwa's position.*

Night came. This time, the voice of "yokai akete" came from the closet in Miwako's room. "Who is it? Is it Kazuyoshi?" called out Miwako.

Emi talked to the voice. "If it's you, Kazuyoshi, tap twice."

After some moments of silence, they heard the voice again saying, "Open it! Open it!" followed by a "tap-tap." Emi was certain that she could communicate with it. But when she opened the closet door, nobody was there.

Emi called out again, "If you're already dead, tap once. If you're still alive, tap twice."

Then, there were two taps. He was either still alive or had already turned into a spirit but thought he was alive and was causing this poltergeist phenomenon. If neither was the case, he might have been brought to another world for some reason. These were the possibilities they could think of.

Emi tried again. "If you're Kazuyoshi, tap twice." There was a response with a "tap-tap." This was somebody with enough intelligence to understand. The question was whether he was of this world or not.

Hikaru chimed in. "Kazuyoshi is nine years old. If you're really Kazuyoshi, you should be able to speak. What's going on?" he said in a strong tone.

"Please help me. I'm trapped in a spider's web. It's dark in here," said the voice.

Now it was clear; this was not a regular kidnapping of this world.

Kazuyoshi was in another world related to aliens.

Principal Reiwa summoned his courage to conduct the ritual "El Cantare Fight" twice and went into a meditative state. Eventually, his son came into spiritual sight; he was caught in the web of a giant poisonous spider.

The aliens must be provoking us. If that's the case, we, too, have an idea, thought the principal.

He called Grand Master Yuho Oyama and reported what had happened.

Yuho Oyama replied, "Your son is trapped in a parallel world. I'll ask Mr. Yaidron, our alien ally, to go and rescue him by creating a wormhole leading to the parallel world. Just give me some time."

Mr. Yaidron accepted Yuho Oyama's request and made his way into the parallel world on his UFO. In the dark world, he found a cave that was covered in the web of a poisonous spider.

He fired four flare shells into the cave. Unable to withstand his attack, the poisonous spider scurried deep into the cave. It was undoubtedly a space creature.

Mr. Yaidron rescued Kazuyoshi safely and brought him back from the parallel world. His UFO landed on the roof of the principal's house. The club supervisors and the rest of the members were called over. A total of seven people from the club gathered at the principal's house.

Mr. Yaidron looked like Superman but had two horns on his head. He was over 6'6" and had an "R.O." mark on his outfit. He turned to Hideo and said, "Get ready. The real battle is about to begin." Then, he was gone in a flash.

Kazuyoshi, who made it home, was in his mother's arms.

"I was so scared," he said.

The principal spoke to Kazuyoshi gently, "I have many enemies. Make sure to thank these young men and women."

The enemies are apparently targeting the HCS Academy. Tough times were approaching. A stern look came over the principal's face.

7.

Hmm, a parallel world.

Principal Reiwa was thinking over a cup of herbal tea in the evening.

What was their goal in getting my son involved in all this? He took another sip of tea. Herbal tea was just right for calming his nerves.

The principal's office was furnished with a chic cupboard, a filing cabinet, and six bookshelves filled with slightly expensive books. Principal Reiwa was a gentleman who once lived in the U.K., so he had no television in his 250-sq. ft. office.

"I'm sure it was a warning to me," he muttered.

They are probably using my family to threaten me so that I would stop the investigation conducted by the UMA Research Club. But I'm an apostle of Light and I cannot abandon my mission. Should anything happen, I will send my children to my wife's parents and protect the Academy at any cost.

The principal moved to the rocking chair and continued to think. It was already past 11 p.m.

The parallel world is a topic of cutting-edge physics. Nobody has ever succeeded in explaining it precisely. But it is said that singularities that are connected to other worlds can be found in various places in this world. At first glance, the parallel world seems similar to the Spirit World, but it seems there is no third-dimensional material or object in the Spirit World. If we were to think of the surface of the Earth as the outer surface of a soccer ball, the parallel world would be its inner surface. It would be dark but still be a third-dimensional-like space. In other words, the parallel world (parallel universe) is a separate world with a different timeline from ours.

For example, if Hitler of Nazi Germany had won World War II, how would the world have unfolded after that? The Cold War between the U.S. and the Soviet Union would never have happened. Neither would the People's Republic of China nor

North Korea have existed. Germany would have been the leader of Europe and the second Holy Roman Empire would have flourished. In that case, the U.S. would have stuck with isolationism, and Japan would have been the one to liberate Asia, Africa, and Latin America.

Or, if Napoleon had not been defeated by Russia and Britain after the French Revolution, France would have become the leader of Europe. In that case, there would have been no Hitler, Mussolini, Lenin, or Stalin. India would have been independent, China would have been divided into French and Japanese blocs, and Canada would have been a French territory.

Alternatively, if Hannibal of Carthage had destroyed the Roman Empire in the three Punic Wars, the center of the world would have been in northern Africa.

Come to think of it, if such scenarios really did unfold in the parallel worlds as part of God's experiment, there would be more than one history of humankind.

But there is another way of looking at the parallel world. It is through the perspective of space, rather than time. It is said that 70 to 80% of the universe is made of dark matter. This means that only the world that was created by light through the Big Bang belongs to the front-side universe, while the majority of the universe still remains in the flip-side universe. From this perspective, civilizations and cultures that were built on religions—which were woven by those referred to as 'gods' or 'Light of Angels'—would be considered very shallow, and the three-dimensional space of the flip-side universe would be the major world. In that case, the beings living in the flip-side universe would return to hell after death as their true home and they would reincarnate between the three-dimensional world and hell. Some evil gods of the dark-side universe, such as Ahriman and Kandahar, actually act on this idea.

Principal Reiwa thought to this extent, but this was the best his brain and enlightenment could take him. He had to ask Grand Master Yuho Oyama of Sun Church for further insight.

Principal Reiwa went to his bedroom and rested his exhausted body for the day.

However, the *shaking* began around 3:00 a.m.

If possible, I'd like a glimpse into the parallel world today, he thought.

He was serious about it; there is no easier way to understand something than through first-hand experience.

His spirit body wandered through a deep forest. He then dove into the deep sea. There was a wide rift in the ocean floor, and his soul fell deep into the earth as the spiraling currents engulfed him. He fell deep down until he saw the ground at the depths of the ocean floor. It was gloomy there. There were many strange creatures. There were also many giant creatures that would have lived if a meteorite with a diameter of 6 miles hadn't fallen on the Yucatán Peninsula 65 million years ago and had not covered the Earth in dust.

Even mammoths, dinosaurs, and pterosaurs existed there.

They seemed to be looking for a singularity (an abnormal point that leads to another world), or a crack in time or space, to get to the Earth's surface.

What would happen if the age of dinosaurs were to coexist with modern civilization? It could happen if the world got warmer as hypothesized. But before that could happen, the creatures of the parallel world might pop out of singularities first.

The soul of Principal Reiwa had a terrifying hour-long experience before finally returning to his bed.

His wife was sound asleep to his left.

The principal sat up and began to pray to Lord God. He knew that prayer was the only way to solve a problem that was beyond his power.

8.

The next incident didn't occur in Inokashira Park where everybody was on the lookout but instead happened in nearby Zempukuji Park.

That day, the pond in Zempukuji Park was bubbling vigorously from the center and creating ripples on the water's surface. Fewer people were strolling around Zempukuji Park compared to Inokashira Park; Zempukuji Park was located in Nishiogi, a residential area in Tokyo.

On the terrace of a café in a glass building, Kohei and Yoko Nagai, a married couple, were having a relaxing time and enjoying their twilight years after retirement.

"There's nothing more I can ask for as long as I can take a walk in this park every now and then and enjoy a nice cup of café au lait in this cafe," said Kohei, as he took a sip from the bowl-shaped cup.

"Don't be silly, my dear," responded his wife Yoko. "You could enjoy taking pictures or painting this beautiful scenery, you know. I've heard that Professor Shoichi Watanabe, who is famous for his book *The Way of Intellectual Life*, and the young Master Ryuho Okawa used to take a walk around this Zempukuji Pond. We, too, should do something meaningful."

Three elementary school students, who were walking by the middle of the pond, were making a fuss as they pointed at the center, where bubbles were bursting out.

"Call the fire department." "No, call the police." The children's voices traveled to the couple in the wind.

"It's wonderful that young people can be so excited about everything," said Kohei.

"I bet those kids will create the future of Japan," replied Yoko.

Then, it happened.

All of a sudden, something like an elephant's head came out of the pond. The children screamed and scampered.

It was coming toward the shore, and its whole body gradually came into sight. It wasn't an elephant. It was a mammoth. What was a mammoth doing in 21st-century Japan?

"Take some pictures, darling. Pictures. Where's your smartphone?"

"I don't have one," Kohei replied to Yoko.

"If we can capture a rare photo, it'll surely be covered as breaking news!" Yoko insisted.

"Maybe we should both get tested for dementia at the hospital," said Kohei.

As the couple was saying this, the mammoth rampaged through the park and out into the town.

The mammoth stampeded through the Nishiogi shopping arcade while stomping on cars and knocking over motorcycles with its trunk. The townspeople froze at the surreal sight.

"Call the police!"

"No, call the zoo!"

"Call the Self-Defense Forces!"

People shouted out for any help they could think of.

Soon a police car arrived, but when they found that it was a 23-foot-long mammoth, they made a U-turn and fled after making a simple radio call.

The mammoth then broke into a grocery store in Nishiogi Town and threw bananas and apples into its mouth using its long trunk. But its tusks were so large that they destroyed many sections of the store.

Before long, the Ueno Zoo employees with tranquilizer guns arrived in a helicopter. They tried to aim at the mammoth from the air but the power lines hindered them from getting close to it.

Then, 20 members of the SAT (Special Assault Team) police unit specializing in counterterrorism arrived. Their mission was to stop the mammoth at any cost before it could break into Nishiogi Station and cause a train accident. Ideally, it should have been captured alive, but the superintendent general issued a shoot-to-kill order because it was destroying many houses. Helicopters from TV Asahi, Nippon Television Network, NHK, and other media outlets were also flying around the area and broadcasting from the air.

The SAT team leader, Toshizo Ishikawa, dispatched automatic rifle squads to separate locations: some in front of the mammoth and others in the narrow paths beside it. He ordered them to fire if it came within 10 yards of them. At the same time, he called out to the residents through the town PA system to evacuate.

A few shots were fired, and the mammoth abruptly charged into the entrance of a condominium.

How could this be? A newly constructed condo with reinforced concrete had a gaping hole and the residents of the 10-story building were taken hostage.

The zoo's tranquilizer gun unit on the ground approached the condo and piled up a mound of bananas on the road in front of the condo. Their plan was to lure the mammoth out of the building.

However, the mammoth used its trunk to suck up a large amount of water from the swimming pool on the condo property and sprayed the water on the tranquilizer gun unit and the SAT members.

The mammoth was over three times more powerful than an ordinary elephant in the zoo. Several people were blasted away.

But then, a mysterious old man appeared. He had a cane, a Dunhill hat on his head, a plaid brown scarf around his neck, and wore an Etro jacket.

The mammoth sprayed water at the old man, as well. But the moment the old man pointed his staff at the mammoth, the water splashed back onto the mammoth's face.

The old man spoke to the mammoth in a loud voice.

"Listen to me well. If you carry on like this, you'll be shot to death. I'll send you home, so return to where you came from."

Saying this, the old man spun the tip of his cane clockwise.

There was a ripping sound as if space were being torn apart. And the mammoth disappeared from the condo as if it had been teleported.

The old man thanked the SAT members for their hard work and disappeared into Nishiogi Station.

"What was that?" a SAT member said.

"Was that old guy a magician?" another said.

The SAT team leader Toshizo Ishikawa explained, "Apparently, to prepare for the worst, the superintendent general has asked Grand Master Yuho Oyama for help."

Everybody in the SAT unit wished that the Self-Defense Forces would take care of the restoration work.

9.

Principal Shohei Reiwa was thinking in the principal's office with his arms crossed.

I think the mammoth that appeared out of Zempukuji Pond was the one I saw during my astral travel to the parallel world. There are two possible explanations for this. One is that somebody—an alien or a god—somehow destroyed or changed the course of the 6-mile-diameter meteorite that was supposed to fall on the Yucatán Peninsula 65 million years ago, and it consequently created at least one world where dinosaurs coexist in the present. The other explanation is that somebody is working to help reveal the secrets of the parallel universe.

Here's another possibility. If the parallel world I saw had a different time and space from ours, it would mean that the multiverse also exists simultaneously. But matters on such a level are way beyond the scope of cutting-edge science; it is so far advanced that it is unclear whether to call it science fiction or the latest studied in physics. It would be the same as the world of the latest "Doctor Strange" movie. Japan doesn't have a Doctor Strange, but we do have Grand Master Yuho Oyama. Perhaps he even surpasses Doctor Strange.

Principal Reiwa spread out a map of Tokyo and gazed at it. *Inokashira Park and Zempukuji Park could be confirmed as "singularities." If so, which park with a pond could be the next "singularity"? The closer it is to central Tokyo, the greater the panic will be. That way, they can make a stronger impression of the parallel universe. In that case…*

Just then, there was a knock on the door of the principal's office. Vice Principal Tatsue Kawaguchi rushed in.

"Sir, an urgent matter has come up. I received a phone call from Ayumu Sakuragawa, Principal of HCS Academy Kansai Campus. He said a Nessie (Loch Ness Monster)-like dinosaur has appeared in Lake Biwa."

The Novel The Shaking

"What? In Lake Biwa? Our Kansai Campus is located near Lake Biwa; it's close enough that the lake can be seen from the school."

"I've heard they already named it 'Biwassie.' According to TV news and other reports, people in the Kansai region are in an uproar. You can also see the news coverage on your smartphone."

Saying this, Tatsue showed him a video on her smartphone. Sure enough, a creature that looked exactly like Nessie was moving across the lake.

Principal Reiwa spoke, "Lake Biwa is not a man-made lake. It was formed in ancient times. Yet, this area on the south side of the lake is evenly deep at 6.5 feet and is highly transparent. The question is whether this monster is swimming with fins or walking on four legs. If it is finned, it won't do much damage beyond tourism and fishing, but if it is four-legged, it could come ashore and endanger the people in our Kansai Campus and the neighboring towns."

"Sir, Hideo Yamakawa, the leader of the UMA Research Group, is here," Tatsue said.

Hideo reported. "Principal, the creature appears to be four-legged. It doesn't seem to be native to Biwa Lake. Much like the incident at Zempukuji Temple, it appeared out of the blue."

"OK. Let's head to the Kansai region," replied the principal. "We have to get to Lake Biwa in Shiga Prefecture. I'll take the five members of the UMA Research Club and the two supervisors with me. We'll leave today and stay there for a week. This will be considered as part of the 'Research and Creative Studies Course'; I'll arrange for the five of you to earn the credits. Get ready for the trip. If there is anything you need, ask the Kansai Campus to prepare it in advance."

"Excuse me, sir," interrupted Setsuko Minami. "My sister is in the Kansai Campus and my home is also in that area. Please let our family assist you, too. In fact, one of our ancestors is Sakata-no-

Kintoki, who is said to be one of the Four Braves that fought and defeated the ogres of Mt. Oe. We also have a secret art of defeating monsters, which has been passed down in our family." She smiled with her big, beady panda-like eyes.

And so, the eight of them headed for the Kansai area. When they got off the bullet train at Kyoto Station, newspaper extras were being handed out on the streets. There were two competing arguments: one said, "Kill Biwassie!" and the other said, "Let's use Biwassie to attract tourists from around the world!"

The eight of them shared a ride in a small cab and a medium-sized van to get to the Happy Christ School (HCS) Kansai Campus, which took them less than an hour.

Ayumu Sakuragawa, the principal of the Kansai Campus, welcomed the group. The members talked about the situation in Tokyo and asked several questions about Biwassie.

"A parallel world? That's amazing," Principal Sakuragawa said.

Principal Reiwa asked him. "Do you think Biwassie should be killed or be used as a tourist attraction?"

"The lake is only 6.5 feet deep, so the creature cannot dive as deep as it could in Loch Ness. I'm sure that sooner or later, it'll attack pleasure boats, fishing boats, and the people on the waterfront. Since it was confirmed to be four-legged, it'll most probably come ashore within a couple of days."

"Are the government and the governor of Shiga Prefecture taking any action?" asked the club leader Hideo.

"They are extremely slow. Our governor is an environmentalist, so he won't do anything unless somebody dies," responded Principal Sakuragawa.

"I think we should eliminate the monster," said Setsuko. "Kyoto and Osaka are bound to suffer great damage soon."

Principal Sakuragawa explained, "The creature is about 65 feet long, but it's still unclear whether it's an herbivore or a carnivore. There's no reason to kill it as long as it only eats fish and other aquatic plants in Lake Biwa. But if the residents start calling for the removal of the dinosaur, the Air, Maritime, and Ground Self-Defense Forces will likely be mobilized and the whole thing will turn into a 'joint exercise.'"

"Please let me fight it," Setsuko insisted. "With the help of my ancestors' power, I'll definitely beat the monster. Unless we defeat it now, the next monster will surely appear."

Supervisor Ishiwatari stepped in, "Let's set up our base in Sun Church's facility, Biwako Shoshinkan, and discuss this further in the evening."

The eight of them moved to Biwako Shoshinkan and had a meeting that night. Setsuko offered herself as a decoy to capture or beat Biwassie.

Emi was worried and said, "Isn't it too dangerous?"

Setsuko answered, "I bet the dinosaur won't be able to resist a beautiful woman, sake barrels, a bonfire, and the smell of roasting meat. It will surely show up at night. We'll lure it in with sake, get it drunk, and lead it into a pit. That's our primary goal. If it's carnivorous, it'll surely go after a panda-like beauty like me, so I'll attract it by standing on a platform and by playing the flute on the stage. And we'll defeat it with the wooden spears set up in a primitive way—just like how the ancient people used to kill wild animals. Let's call this 'Operation Yamata-no-Orochi (legendary eight-headed serpent)'."

The boys insisted that they didn't want to put a girl in danger, but Setsuko was determined. "Unless somebody gets hurt, the Self-Defense Forces and the police won't take any action, and public opinion won't change, either," she said. She really was a descendant of an ogre exterminator after all.

A dangerous gamble was about to begin.

10.

Setsuko's suggestion was approved, and the operation to capture Biwassie began.

The club leader Hideo arranged for a contractor to start digging a hole in the most suitable location on the sandy beach of Lake Biwa.

Hikaru and Jiro built a bamboo tower with the help of the students from the HCS Kansai Campus. They decided that the best height of the tower was about 26 feet, based on the estimated length of Biwassie's neck. They added a 118 sq. ft. wooden stage—or dance floor—on top of the tower. This was a request from Setsuko. They set up a Japanese drum and circular sleigh bells on the wooden stage. Setsuko's plan was to attract Biwassie's attention with the drums and to ring the bells to attract it closer to her once it was on the shore.

Emi ordered eight sake barrels and lined them up along the shoreline. She was preparing to crack the lids open in the evening.

Feeling excited about "Operation Capture Yamata-no-Orochi," the locals also helped the club members.

"Let's capture it alive and keep it in a cage at the zoo in Kyoto," a young man from the local youth group said with much excitement.

Hideo also secretly arranged for high-speed motorboats, divers, and underwater guns without letting Setsuko know just in case of an emergency.

Setsuko was planning to dance to the "Princess Konohana-no-Sakuyabime" song on the stage, so she prepared the vestments of a shrine maiden.

Hideo prepared 20 bamboo spears with the help of some carpenters. He also arranged for four members of a hunting club in Shiga Prefecture to bring their tranquilizer guns, also in case of an emergency.

Now, the question was whether Biwassie would actually drink sake like the serpent Yamata-no-Orochi did, become drunk, approach Setsuko on the wooden stage, and successfully be led to fall into the pit.

At the suggestion of Mr. Ishiwatari the club supervisor, they also prepared a crane truck to be parked 10 yards behind the wooden stage. It was equipped with a translucent wire rope that would be extended to Setsuko and tied around her waist so that she could be pulled away in case the operation was deemed too dangerous.

Biwassie was now half a mile away, craning its neck and showing its Godzilla-like dorsal fins.

It was uncertain if this dinosaur would respond to meat, but they prepared poultry, beef, pork, and fish, among other types of meat, and began grilling them on the beach. They had also ordered some fresh kelp in case it was an herbivore; they planned to grill it until it turned to ashes.

Everything was ready. They were also ready to record the whole operation on video. The only thing left to do now was to play the "Yamata-no-Orochi" song on the CD player and have Principal Reiwa use his telekinesis to attract the mysterious creature.

The operation began at 7:00 p.m.

Biwassie slowly and steadily approached the shore over the course of 30 minutes as everybody watched it with bated breath. But Biwassie stopped when it was about 10 yards from the beach.

Ms. Yamaoka, a female science teacher and a supervisor of the UMA Research Club, murmured, "For an ancient dinosaur, it's more cautious and intelligent than I thought. I wonder if it has evolved in the last million years."

The dinosaur didn't come straight toward Setsuko, who was dancing under the spotlight on the stage that was 26 feet tall. It was sensing some kind of a trap. Contrary to everybody's expectations, the dinosaur moved in a parallel direction, along the beach, for about 55 yards before it came ashore.

It then turned in the direction of Setsuko and began plodding toward her, as if to mock human intelligence; it would neither fall for bait nor into a pit.

Soon enough, Biwassie knocked over the bamboo tower. The wire rope that was supposed to pull Setsuko back somehow became untied, and Biwassie caught her in its mouth. Setsuko's shriek pierced through the dark night. The dinosaur moved on for another 55 yards without paying attention to everybody on the shore and splashed back into the darkness of Lake Biwa.

It was a complete strategic failure. The dinosaur had already moved 110 yards away. Fortunately, the flashing light and the location transmitter attached to Setsuko were still functioning.

Setsuko's younger sister Yumiko (9th grade) was shouting her sister's name.

Without anybody noticing, the freelance journalist Tosuke Ishikura was recording the entire incident on his smartphone.

Eight men with bamboo spears boarded two high-speed motorboats and set off to search for Setsuko. They were the three male students from the Research Club, and a few local fishermen and underwater divers.

When the dinosaur was half a mile away, Setsuko's light went out. They couldn't tell if she was alive or dead. The signal of her location transmitter stopped at the same spot, but Biwassie was nowhere to be seen.

Principal Reiwa said, "This can't be happening! I thought it appeared from the parallel world by chance, but apparently, it can also return there at will. If Setsuko was taken away to a world full of dinosaurs, how can we possibly help her out?"

There was nothing they could do except to report her missing to the police.

Meanwhile, the freelance journalist Tosuke uploaded a video on the Internet with the title, "The Terrifying Academy: Operation No Regard for Human Life," and started to spread it. In it, he warned about the cult-like nature of the UMA Research Club. He will likely write articles in gossip magazines to accuse the Academy next.

The major newspapers ran a short story in their Shiga Prefecture editions with the picture of Biwassie taking Setsuko away.

However, now that Biwassie—the very culprit—had disappeared from Lake Biwa, it was impossible to investigate the case. Underwater divers looked for the body of Setsuko, but even that was nowhere to be found.

11.

The search in Lake Biwa was called off. Some volunteer fishermen and police officers continued to patrol the lake every day, but the UMA Research Club members decided to leave Shiga Prefecture and return home for now. When they arrived at Kyoto Station in Kyoto Prefecture, which is next to Shiga Prefecture, there was a huge commotion going on there, as well.

Centuries ago, the warlord Nobunaga Oda was attacked by his subordinate Mitsuhide Akechi when he was staying at Honno-ji Temple with only 50 men. In the end, Nobunaga set fire to his lodging and fell on his own sword. Mitsuhide then ruled the country, which was short-lived; he was defeated by Hideyoshi Toyotomi, who quickly returned from Okayama to avenge his master. Hideyoshi then became the ruler of the country, which marked the beginning of the new era.

However, some historians think that it should have been impossible for Nobunaga, who was a man of great foresight, to be defeated so easily by a rebellion. They believe that Japan would have been revolutionized much sooner had Nobunaga's reign continued; as a result, Japan wouldn't have closed its borders and Japan's westernization would have started 300 years earlier.

Principal Reiwa and his team picked up a newspaper extra here in Kyoto, again. The extra said that an underground passageway had suddenly opened below Honno-ji Temple, and 1,000 of Nobunaga's horsemen had appeared out of the ground.

Common sense was shaking.

According to the news, Nobunaga and his troops fled as they killed several policemen with spears and bow-and-arrows before they holed themselves up in Kiyomizu-dera Temple.

Hideo and Jiro pressed the principal for an answer. "What should we do, sir?" they asked.

After discussing the matter with the two supervisors, Principal Reiwa said, "We decided to take this opportunity as a special historical research class. We'll stay at a cheap business hotel in front of Kyoto Station and conduct a follow-up investigation on Nobunaga and his men at Kiyomizu-dera Temple for just three days. Unless we do this, it may be hard to solve the mystery surrounding Setsuko."

And so, the seven members moved toward Kiyomizu-dera Temple. The riot police were already on guard. Mr. Ishiwatari, the club supervisor and a fifth-degree black belt holder in kendo, was eager to find out who was stronger, a samurai of the Warring States period or himself in the present day.

Club leader Hideo, a second-degree black belt holder in kendo, was also excited to beat at least two or three samurai. Hikaru, a second-degree black belt holder in karate, and Jiro, the runner-up in the Tokyo Metropolitan High School Boxing

Kiyomizu-dera Temple

The stage of Kiyomizu

Championship, were very enthusiastic as well. Nobody knew this, but the female student Emi was also strong; she had a second-degree black belt in aikido.

The principal and the club supervisors decided to be in charge of making the overall decision and negotiating with Nobunaga. The students and Mr. Ishiwatari got dressed for the fight in their respective gear: kendo uniforms with wooden swords, boxing gloves and headgear, karate uniform, and gym clothes. They all approached Kiyomizu-dera Temple as close as they could in a large van.

According to the city people they met on the slope leading to Kiyomizu-dera Temple, Nobunaga had proclaimed himself as the shogun, or Commander-in-Chief, and declared Kyoto as his capital. Apparently, historians and others were using the microphone and built-in speakers of a police car to convince him that the times shifted to the era of Hideyoshi and that of Ieyasu after he was assassinated. They also tried to inform him that he was currently in the modern era, which came after the Meiji period. But Nobunaga wouldn't lend an ear and said, "Mitsuhide defeating me? That's nonsense. And Hideyoshi is no more than my sandal bearer." He seemed to believe that he had broken through Mitsuhide's encirclement and had moved to Kiyomizu-dera Temple instead.

Riot police captain Shochoku Nambara was not sure what to do. Should he ask the prime minister to negotiate with Nobunaga? Or should he have the historians decide how history should unfold? Should the capital be moved from Tokyo to Kyoto? In that case, should the emperor and empress also move to the Kyoto Imperial Palace?

Nobunaga's men shot fire arrows at the Asahi Shimbun newspaper helicopter that was flying around Kiyomizu-dera Temple. They killed the pilot, so the helicopter crashed. The NHK helicopter retreated to higher skies.

The mayor of Kyoto spoke to them on the microphone, too, but it was no use.

Mr. Ishiwatari with a fifth-degree black belt in kendo and the club leader Hideo, a second-degree holder, seized the opportunity and rushed into the temple with their wooden swords.

"We bring you reinforcements! Let us assist you!" shouted Mr. Ishiwatari in classical Japanese. He was a history teacher at the HCS Academy, so he was also well-versed in the old language. The two approached the main camp. Because they were carrying wooden swords, nobody suspected them.

Ranmaru Mori, Nobunaga's head pageboy, walked over using a spear as a cane.

"You. What do you want?" Ranmaru asked them.

"We've come to serve you as your strategists. You seem confused about the current situation of Kiyomizu-dera Temple." Mr. Ishiwatari said.

"Indeed. Large mechanical dragonflies (helicopters) are flying in the sky and the townspeople are wearing strange clothes. I recognize parts of the temple, but the townspeople's houses resemble foreign buildings. The guards (referring to the riot police) are carrying foreign-made matchlock guns, and there are many transparent box-like ox carts running around the town. The ground has no dirt and is hard like stone," Ranmaru said.

"In a nutshell, you've come to the future—to a much later world. A world that is 500 years in the future."

"Half of what you say makes no sense, but I can understand the other half. You mean, God or Buddha is showing Lord Nobunaga the future world, don't you? It's not surprising for such a thing to happen because our lord is the incarnation of God or Buddha. There are some insane people over there shouting that our lord was killed by *that* Mitsuhide. Can't you do something about them?"

"Now that you are in a future society, there must be many misunderstandings."

"So you are the strategist, and is the young one next to you your apprentice?"

Hideo chimed in. "That's right, sir. I believe it would be wise to accept my master's offer. Otherwise, you'll all be beaten by the Western-style army over there."

"Are you folks from the future that strong? Somebody! Come here and test the abilities of this boy and his master with a wooden sword."

The sword instructor Kyogoku stepped forward to challenge Hideo with a wooden sword. Unfortunately, Hideo was struck in the body on the fifth move. Next, the instructor went up against Mr. Ishiwatari, a fifth-degree black belt holder. Mr. Ishiwatari held out for about three minutes but surrendered when he had the tip of the instructor's sword held at his throat.

Emi ran toward them with a worried look. Seeing that she was a girl, nobody stood on their guard.

Emi made sure the two were safe.

Then, from behind her, instructor Kyogoku tapped her right shoulder with his left hand.

At that moment, Emi grabbed his left arm and threw him onto the ground by using a special aikido technique called a "vacuum throw." To his shame, Kyogoku fell flat on his back on the cobblestones and was unconscious for five seconds.

"What a splendid ninja." Ranmaru applauded. "You could be of use. You said you brought reinforcements. Bring your men here."

The seven members of the Research Club met with Nobunaga.

Principal Reiwa introduced himself as the captain.

"Show me what you can do," demanded Nobunaga. So Principal Reiwa had Nobunaga's favorite candelabra placed 33 feet away from him and had the seven candles lit. He then knelt down on one knee, closed his eyes, put his hands together, and focused his mind on the candles. The flames of the candles swayed side to side, and all seven candles went out.

"Brilliant! I like it," said Nobunaga.

What should we do next? Everybody in the Research Club thought hard.

12.

Nobunaga then took an interest in Jiro's headgear and gloves.

"Bring me Monk Nittai, the stick fighter, and have him fight that one with puffy gloves (Jiro) on the stage of Kiyomizu," ordered Nobunaga.

Monk Nittai came forward carrying an 8-foot-long wooden stick with a piece of cloth wrapped around its end. He swung the stick around wildly and sometimes jabbed it into Jiro straight on. Jiro, the boxer, dodged the stick from side to side, or by occasionally lowering his head.

"How cheeky!" shouted the monk and swung his stick down. Jiro jumped and dodged it. Then, he closed in on the monk and threw a left and right hook, followed by an uppercut. The monk staggered backward.

Jiro didn't miss this opportunity to land four body blows on the monk. Finally, the monk fell flat on his back, foaming at the mouth.

"Splendid!" said Ranmaru. "The people from the future are strong, indeed."

Next, Hikaru, a second-degree black belt holder in karate, was called up.

He was matched against Toranosuke Takai, a master of the sickle chain.

Toranosuke held the sickle in his left hand as he spun the chain with a weight attached to it in his right hand. If the chain ever wrapped around Hikaru's body, he would be tugged in and beheaded with the sickle.

The entire event was televised live throughout Japan under the title, "The Great Battle on the Stage of Kiyomizu" from the NHK news helicopter.

The NHK reporter commented, "The boxer from the earlier battle secured a win against the medieval stick fighter. The next opponent is a sickle chain user. Can the high school karate fighter beat him?"

Hikaru dodged the first swinging weight attack but it was soon followed by another shot. The flying weight dug into the wooden board. Hikaru then hopped onto the taut chain and took a few steps before landing a spinning kick to the back of Toranosuke's head with his left foot. Seeing Toranosuke lose balance, Hikaru delivered a heel drop to the top of Toranosuke's head with his right foot.

"Enough." Nobunaga halted the fight. "You future people have proven yourselves enough. Your techniques were all new to me."

Nobunaga was in good spirits. He then looked at the female biology teacher, Ms. Teruko Yamaoka, and said, "She, too, must have some special abilities."

Principal Reiwa got flustered. "She's well versed in animals and ancient creatures, but she's not a fighter."

Ms. Yamaoka interrupted, "All I need to do is show you some tricks, right? I'm a science teacher at a high school now, but I used to study hypnotherapy in medical school. Let me demonstrate a group hypnosis on you, Lord Nobunaga, along with your close aides."

She asked Nobunaga and his men to come a little closer to her. She then took out a gold pocket watch from her inner pocket attached to a 12-inch gold chain.

"Lord Nobunaga and gentlemen, please focus your attention on this gold watch."

Saying so, she began to swing the gold watch from side to side like a pendulum.

"The clouds will begin to loom over the sky at once."

As she said so, dark clouds suddenly filled the sky, which was clear until then. Lightning started to flash.

"Next, a dragon will appear out of the clouds."

Exactly as she said, a legendary dragon appeared from the black clouds.

"This dragon breathes fire."

The fire dragon blew fire as it flew around Kiyomizu-dera Temple.

Fire broke out in various parts of Kiyomizu-dera Temple, and the entire temple was ablaze. Nobunaga's troops began to flee and jump off the stage of Kiyomizu one after another. The temple was engulfed in a raging fire.

Strangely enough, the warriors who jumped off the stage vanished out of sight.

By the time 50 of them had disappeared, those in Nobunaga's main camp began to panic in fear.

"I didn't know there was such a priestess who could command a fire dragon. I am stunned. We surrender, we surrender," said Nobunaga.

Seeing this, the riot police captain Shochoku Nambara ordered his unit to charge in.

"We are no match for the people of the future." Saying so, Nobunaga and his men dropped their weapons in defeat and were detained in the police van.

However, after the van had been on the road for a while, the warriors' bodies gradually became translucent and faded away.

Before long, all of Nobunaga's troops were gone. Kiyomizu-dera Temple reappeared from out of the flames. The dark clouds also disappeared and the fire dragon flew away high into the sky.

Kyoto was restored to its current, 21st-century state.

Principal Reiwa told Ms. Yamaoka, "That was amazing. You must have been a shaman in ancient times."

Captain Nambara politely thanked the seven of them.

Mr. Ishiwatari said, "All right. Now, shall we analyze Biwassie and the phenomenon of Nobunaga's troops on our way home? Let's go back to Tokyo."

Setsuko's younger sister, Yumiko, transferred to the HCS Tokyo Campus and joined the UMA

Research Club to continue investigating her sister's whereabouts.

13.

Everybody was thinking the same thing on the bullet train back to Tokyo and back at the school in Tokyo. Nobody believed that Setsuko was dead. They knew she had been taken to a parallel world along with Biwassie. They needed to figure out a rescue plan or find a way to get to the parallel world.

The details regarding the result of the operation at Lake Biwa were still being spread as "News on the Terrifying Academy" by Tosuke Ishikura, a freelance journalist who preyed on religion.

On the other hand, the Research Club also received a lot of support and encouragement from the general public, who saw their battles at Kiyomizu-dera Temple broadcast live by NHK. Day by day, more and more people were calling out to them, "Please save Japan!" or "Save our future!"

Hideo, being aware of his responsibility as the club leader, was thinking in his room. Setsuko's sister, Yumiko, kept insisting, "If it takes too long, my sister's life will be in danger." He, too, was more than well aware of that. Yumiko used to belong to the kyudo (Japanese archery) club at the Kansai Campus, so she was preparing a bow and arrow and a stone spear that a caveman would have used to kill dinosaurs in the prehistoric era. She believed beating Biwassie in the same way that cavemen in the age of dinosaurs fought would bring about the same result as the incident at Kiyomizu-dera Temple and enable Setsuko to come back to this world from *that* world.

Hideo thought that they should start by exploring the secrets of the Greys and their UFOs that appeared in Inokashira Park, as well as their relationship with the flip-side universe. After all, that was where it all started. The mammoth in Zempukuji Park, the incident at Lake Biwa, and finally, the appearance of Nobunaga all happened subsequently, so the key had to lie in the very first incident.

What's more, he thought, *all the incidents are connected to our UMA Research Club, as well. If so, somebody must be watching the series of incidents. If we're being monitored, there must also be a way to trace back to them. I bear responsibility as the club leader, so I could be taken to where Setsuko is if that's what it takes.*

Hideo knew that the location transmitter attached to Setsuko was still working and that it was now moving from Lake Biwa to Tokyo. Whether she was alive or dead was uncertain, but at least he knew Setsuko's physical body, which was in another dimension, was approaching Tokyo. It was highly likely that Biwassie would appear out of a body of water in the vicinity of Tokyo. Even if it didn't, somebody had to go and help Setsuko anyway. Her younger sister Yumiko was thinking of beating the 65-foot dinosaur with a bow and arrow. Hideo had noticed she was even more of a pure physical fighter than her sister.

Although Operation Yamata-no-Orochi failed, the chance of our succeeding must have been at least 50% if Biwassie only had the intelligence of an ancient creature. This time, we don't need to beat it. As long as we can get Setsuko back alive, there won't be any problem with Biwassie swimming in the Fuji Five Lakes; we'll settle for a draw, he thought.

Hideo called a meeting.

"We'll try to track down the Greys again and look for the small insect-like robot. I'm sure it's watching us from somewhere."

This was the club leader's suggestion. Hikaru and Jiro took the lead in searching for the "insect" in the vicinity of the school. As summer vacation was approaching, there were many insects at this time of year, so it was surprisingly difficult to identify the one they were looking for.

In the meantime, Emi and Yumiko installed infrared cameras on the roof of the school and on the roof of the principal's house.

A few days later, Hikaru found a male beetle perched on the screen door of the club room. To avoid repeating the previous mistake, this time, he carefully and gently caught it and put it in his insect cage.

When the club members scanned it with a metal detector, the signal from the detector confirmed their suspicion that it was a small alien robot.

"It'd be great if we can somehow capture a Grey. I wish they'd come looking for this beetle." This was Hideo's plan.

Emi reported on the camera footage. "The infrared camera on the roof of the principal's house captured a video of something that moved like a *kappa* and also an image of a small UFO."

"How can we catch a Grey?"

The five of them discussed. According to the information they collected on monsters so far, Greys can freely pass through walls like ghosts. Perhaps Greys have the ability to create inter-dimensional tunnels. If so, they can easily escape any traps, such as cages or metal boxes. Was there any way to persuade them to guide the club members to the parallel world? If the Greys were really going in and out of the parallel worlds, why were they doing so in the first place?

Supervisor Yamaoka, the female biology teacher, spoke. "Suppose they visit Earth on UFOs. If multidimensional worlds really do exist and different civilizations are flourishing in each world, it would be valuable work to compare, analyze, and report on them. Especially, for somebody like me who studies living creatures from both ancient time and modern times, that would be precious information."

At that moment, the small beetle-robot in the insect cage spread its wings several times as if to fly.

"Maybe it means 'yes'," said Hideo.

"Perhaps we can use this beetle-robot to talk to its owner," suggested Yumiko. Then she asked a question.

"Mr. Beetle, Mr. Beetle. Is my sister, Setsuko, still alive?"

The beetle's abdomen flashed like a firefly.

Ms. Yamaoka said, "That must also mean 'yes.' The beetle's eyes must be sending images and its horns information. Maybe we can talk to its owner."

Yumiko asked another question, "Mr. Beetle, Mr. Beetle. Will you help us bring my sister back?"

The beetle didn't respond.

Hideo spoke, "I guess we'll have to ask Principal Reiwa to go on an interdimensional trip tonight."

At that moment, the beetle went up in smoke with a "pow."

14.

Upon receiving the students' request, Principal Reiwa offered a prayer for a successful interdimensional trip to find Setsuko.

That night, he did not sleep in his usual bedroom but in a different one with a Japanese sword in his arms. He, too, used to be a member of the kendo club at Kaisei Junior and Senior High School and was a third-degree black belt holder. He slightly regretted that he wasn't matched against anybody at Kiyomizu-dera Temple. With his Japanese sword, he could beat any opponent be it a poisonous spider or Biwassie in the parallel world. Nobody would complain even if he killed those creatures to rescue Setsuko.

When Principal Reiwa was sleeping on the couch in his office with a Japanese sword in his arms, *it* began at a little past 3:00 a.m. His toes began to tremble and his right hand—

the one that was not holding the sword—also began to shake. His left hand was gripping the Japanese sword tightly so that he could surely take it with him.

The principal's spirit body slowly sat up. His left hand was firmly holding the Japanese sword, which was imbued with the samurai spirit.

His soul plunged into the depths of the deep water as if he were scuba diving. The water current began to swirl like a whirlpool. But he was not suffering from a lack of oxygen. Of course, he wasn't—he was a spirit after all.

Eventually, he broke through the bottom of the lake and found a primitive landscape unfolding before his eyes. Looking at the vast field of reeds and a lake, he had a sense of déjà vu. He understood that Lake Biwa in the parallel world had moved underneath Tokyo.

As he glanced around, he noticed Yumiko ahead of him on the right, crouching down in the reeds and moving forward. Apparently, her strong love for her big sister made it possible for her to astral travel in the middle of the night.

After walking for a while, he found Biwassie resting on the shore. Setsuko was also there; she seemed to be sleeping on the dinosaur's back.

What should I do now? The principal wondered for a moment.

But even before 30 seconds had passed, Yumiko drew her bow and shot an arrow into Biwassie's right eye. Biwassie abruptly shook its head, but the arrow wouldn't fall out. It turned its head toward the two. Yumiko took a second shot and hit Biwassie in the left eye. She was a skilled sharpshooter. She was no doubt a descendant of Kintoki Sakata and the champion at the Kansai Archery Competition.

Biwassie came charging toward her and the principal even though it couldn't see; it could track them based on their human scent.

For some reason, Setsuko was still lying face down on the dinosaur's back, as if she were glued to it.

Principal Reiwa thought he should not allow Biwassie to escape into the lake; he thought he should lead the creature toward the shore and make it charge and attack them instead.

When he looked over to Yumiko, she had already launched her next attack. She threw a spear with a stone arrowhead at Biwassie's throat. It struck the dinosaur right in the neck and pierced through it.

"What amazing precision!" The principal was astounded.

Even though Biwassie was now blind, they knew the operation would fail if they let it escape into the lake. Principal Reiwa provoked the dinosaur by mimicking a battle cry like that of the Apache tribe, quickly covering and uncovering his mouth with his right hand. It rushed toward him as blood streamed down from both of its eyes.

He jumped up, flipped once in the air, and landed on the base of Biwassie's neck. His body felt light for some reason. Of course, it did—he was a spirit after all. He then drew his legendary sword and cut through the dinosaur's neck. Biwassie's neck was only 18 inches in diameter even though its body was 65 feet long. They could tell it was herbivorous based on the shape of its teeth.

Biwassie's head fell to the ground and the dinosaur collapsed to its knees in a heap.

The principal ran up the dinosaur's back. Setsuko was still alive, although she had grown very weak.

"Oh, good. Thank God."

As he gently lowered Setsuko off the dinosaur's back, her sister Yumiko ran over and hugged her.

"Sis, it's me, Yumiko. I'm here to rescue you," said Yumiko.

"Thank you—thank you for coming." Setsuko managed to answer as she panted.

The principal spoke, "Keep holding each other tightly. I'll transfer you both to our living room."

He concentrated his mind using what little energy he had left in him and transferred them back home using telekinesis.

The Minami sisters appeared in the living room of the principal's house. Sensing this, the principal's wife, Mitsuko, awoke and came to the living room.

She brought bath towels and bathrobes and looked after Setsuko.

Soon the other members of the club received the message and gathered at the principal's house.

The club leader Hideo said, "So, the rescue operation was a success."

Yumiko recounted the battle against Biwassie to everybody.

"By the way, has the principal come back yet?" Jiro remarked.

"He'll be back soon." Everybody was confident and optimistic.

More than anything, they were happy to see Setsuko back safe and sound after she had been taken away for several days.

Meanwhile, contrary to their expectations, Principal Reiwa had exhausted his mental energy and was catching his breath by Biwassie's side. He was still holding the bloody sword in his right hand.

Then, all of a sudden, a spider's thread flew out of nowhere and wrapped around his spirit body.

It pulled him toward the mountain as it made a whizzing sound.

It was the same poisonous spider that kidnapped his son Kazuyoshi the other day. Was it holding a grudge because Kazuyoshi was rescued successfully?

Principal Reiwa was dragged into a cave in the mountain.

Everybody had begun to worry because he hadn't returned even after an hour had passed.

Miwako, the principal's 11-year-old daughter who was sensitive to spiritual matters, conducted remote viewing.

"Oh no, Dad has been captured by the poisonous spider just like Kazuyoshi was," she said.

Another serious problem had befallen them.

15.

The eight members of the UMA Research Club got together at the principal's house. The principal's family and the school doctor were also there.

Dr. Daikichi Kamo, who was 50 years old, examined the principal's physical body, which now lay in his bedroom.

"If you take him to the hospital, he'll be declared dead. His heart isn't beating and he's not breathing. But as the HCS Academy doctor, I'd say that his soul is out of his body now and is undergoing astral travel. The question is how long his physical body will last in this state. Plato's *Republic* has a story of a young man named Er, who was dead for days before coming back to life in the second week just as he was about to be cremated on his funeral pyre. It is said he then told an account of the other world. Based on this story, I suppose two weeks would be the maximum. Swedenborg, a Scandinavian psychic, holds the record for astral traveling for one week. Since it's summer now, the body will be damaged easily, so please place ice packs around the principal's bed and keep the temperature around his body between 50 and 60°F. The hospital would immediately pronounce him dead, so all we can do is to pray that he comes back to life," the school doctor explained.

It takes a lot of patience for those who wait the return of a spirit to its body. Even though it took a week to rescue Setsuko, she had now regained her spirit and was full of energy again. She prayed for the safe return of Principal Reiwa, who had saved her life. Her sister Yumiko prayed the same.

Everybody wondered. *Is the principal fighting the poisonous spider now? Can he escape on his own? Does he need help? According to what Yumiko said, the principal was strong enough to cut off Biwassie's head with the legendary Japanese sword, Kotetsu, so there would be no better reinforcement than the principal himself. Kotetsu is a masterpiece that can even cut through other Japanese swords; it was the favorite sword of the famous 19th-century swordsman Isami Kondo of Shinsengumi, as well. Yumiko is quite certain that Principal Reiwa didn't let go of it even though he's trapped in a poisonous spider's web. He'll most certainly fight back once he recovers his energy and strength.*

On top of that, the principal's daughter Miwako saw him through remote viewing and he said, "Don't come over here to help me. It is a teacher's mission to help the students. If my life is what it costs to kill this creature, I'll gladly give it up."

Meanwhile, in a cave in the mountains of the parallel world, although his spirit was trapped in a giant spider web, Principal Reiwa was in thought.

Although the level of my enlightenment is still low, I've come to have this strong supernatural power, thanks to the guidance of Grand Master Yuho Oyama. So, rather than simply saving myself, I want to reveal the truth about this poisonous spider and the secrets of the parallel world even a little. Transcending life and death is the starting point of Bushido, he thought.

While his movement was restricted by the spider's thread that had bound him tightly, he was regaining his ability to think.

The spider's web was about 40 feet in diameter. The tarantula that captured him was about 26 feet long. For the sake of the club's further research, he thought he needed to confirm whether this was the only poisonous spider that existed here.

He was regaining his spiritual power. The prayers of the club members were also reaching him and giving him the power of courage.

Principal Reiwa found that the spider that captured him was called "Queen Moon." Apparently, it had been remotely guiding Sun Myung Moon, the founder of the Unification Church, and his wife for decades. Their goal was to take over Japan and turn it into a vassal state of Korea as the "Land of Eve." They wanted to create a unified Korea and reign over it as the "Land of Adam." The soul of Sun Myung Moon, too, has now taken the form of a poisonous spider in a cave of the Abysmal Hell within the Earth's Spirit World. He also wields influence on people on earth, and more than 10 Japanese Diet members seem to have become entangled in his webs in the Spirit World.

Principal Reiwa's spiritual vision showed him another large poisonous spider called "King Kim" in a different cave deeper in the mountains. It was a tarantula that provided remote spiritual guidance to the three generations of North Korean leaders. This 42-foot-long tarantula was the one that made Kim Il-sung what he was. Kim Il-sung, the founder of North Korea, also fell into the depths of hell after death and transformed into a tarantula in another cave of the Abysmal Hell.

King Kim also guided the next two successive leaders: Kim Jong-il and Kim Jong-un. The root of the North Korean threat of nuclear development and ballistic missiles lay here.

What is more, because the poisonous spiders in the parallel world are aliens, the angels of the Earth's Spirit World cannot easily interfere. This is the reality of the Korean Peninsula from a spiritual point of view. Principal Reiwa had no regrets about fighting to the death against these poisonous spiders—or aliens—and dying in the line of duty if it meant protecting the Academy, his home country Japan, and bringing true peace to the world.

If I can save millions of lives and deter a nuclear war, my life is a small price to pay, he thought.

But there was no way these spiders existed independently; they were definitely colluding with other malicious aliens.

He calmed his breath and concentrated his mind deeply to further refine his spiritual ability.

Just as I expected, the pond of Inokashira Park has become a singularity through which living beings of the dark-side universe have access to this parallel world. So, the opening of the HCS Academy near Inokashira Park was very bad news for them. It meant that their evil deeds would be unveiled and watched.

The principal awakened to his mission.

If I can defeat Queen Moon that is holding me captive, I can save Japanese politics. And if I can defeat King Kim, I can prevent the outbreak of nuclear war that may arise between the Korean Peninsula and Japan. In the worst-case scenario, I must ask for the help of Grand Master Yuho Oyama, but what can I do on my own? Now is the time to die for the Truth, he thought.

He bid farewell to his wife and his children in his heart.

Goodbye, my love. I want to leave behind the spirit of self-sacrifice for the sake of my students in the Academy.

Back in the bedroom where his body lay, Miwako, his eldest daughter, relayed his thoughts to everybody there.

16.

The huge spider crept up on Principal Reiwa. It came to see how worn out he had become. If he appeared weak enough, it would probably stab him with its poisonous fangs, gobble him up, and absorb his anima (life energy).

Principal Reiwa pretended to be unconscious. As the giant spider approached him, it blew out its rancid breath. It was the smell of a morgue.

The eight-legged spider stabbed him in the side with its left front claw. Blood trickled down from the left side of the principal's body, even though he was a spirit and should not be bleeding.

The principal's physical body on earth also started bleeding from a stab mark that appeared on his left side. Everybody there screamed in surprise. His wife Mitsuko shook his shoulders and cried out, "Are you all right?"

Principal Reiwa was thinking. *Even though it appears to be a poisonous spider, it must be an alien. It would be the first experiment for humankind to see which counterattacks work on aliens and which spiritual powers have no effect.*

Next, the tarantula used its right front claw to stab the principal, who was entangled in its thread. It made another wound on the right side, making more blood drip. A stab mark also appeared on the right side of his body on earth, causing blood to flow out.

Hideo, Hikaru, and Jiro were furious.

"Is there any way for us to go to the parallel world?" "How was Yumiko able to get there?"

Yumiko looked around and said, "I was desperate to save my sister."

But Miwako, the principal's daughter, calmed them and explained, "Dad keeps saying that he doesn't want to endanger his students' lives. He probably has an idea."

Hideo insisted, "But these stab marks and bleeding definitely mean that he's being attacked by the tarantula."

So once again, they all prayed for the spider's thread to break.

A few strands of thread that were binding the principal's hands and legs snapped.

Principal Reiwa turned his body around and used his beloved sword to sever the tarantula's two front claws.

The tarantula let out a strange squeal and jumped back about three feet. The principal stood on the ground of the dark cave.

His Japanese sword sparkled as he slashed down at the tarantula's mouth. But at the same moment, the tarantula also spat six strands of sticky white thread from its mouth. Principal Reiwa's sword was just short of cutting off Queen Moon's beak.

The principal pulled his sword back, and this time, began to destroy the webs in the cave. He cut off all the thick thread attached to the walls, one after another. The tarantula crawled back along the thread that led deeper into the cave.

But then, out of the sticky ground of the cave, several huge worm-like tentacles emerged and they wrapped around his legs and lower body. He sliced off the tops of some of the worms' heads.

Suddenly, he heard a voice.

"That's enough."

He was surprised to see Grand Master Yuho Oyama standing beside him, holding an umbrella as a walking stick.

"You did quite well," said Grand Master Oyama. "But your enemy is a space creature that can freely shape-shift at will. Its true form isn't just a poisonous spider. What appears to be a cave here is just one of many passageways to its UFO. I think it's my turn to fight."

Grand Master Oyama opened his umbrella and spun it around. Then, a rainbow-colored light scattered inside the cave.

A sizzling sound came from the tarantula's respiratory organ, and smoke billowed out.

Next, Grand Master Oyama folded his umbrella and pointed its tip at the tarantula. Then, a spiritual ray resembling lightning shot out.

Queen Moon was charred, and the next moment, it shrank to about three feet in size.

Principal Reiwa spoke, "Master, this is our chance to finish it off."

But Grand Master Oyama replied, "No, I'm afraid I wouldn't do that. If I do, this whole cave will turn into a UFO and take us into the deep recesses of the dark-side universe. The best way to win here is to escape."

Saying so, Grand Master Oyama stuck his umbrella into the ground.

A hole about three feet wide suddenly emerged.

"Come on, let's get out of here." Grand Master Oyama jumped down into the hole.

Principal Reiwa had no other choice but to follow him.

They landed on a rock surface. As they ran toward the grassy field, what appeared to be mountains began to transform. Soon, two large black saucer-shaped UFOs appeared.

Oyama explained, "Those UFOs are the command ships that are manipulating South Korea and North Korea. Destroying them completely would invite a Korean War of devastation on earth. It is a matter that calls for a discussion with the superior aliens and also the gods of America. So it is a matter beyond your duties. It seems like you're a bit injured. You should return home safely now for the sake of your family and everybody in the Research Club."

Then, a tornado emerged. It swirled around Principal Reiwa and lifted him upward.

Grand Master Yuho Oyama waved his Dunhill hat to see him off.

The principal's body that lay in his bedroom came back to life.

"Are you all right?" asked his wife Mitsuko.

"I guess I am," the principal replied.

"Grand Master Oyama came to rescue Dad at just the right time," Miwako said.

"I would've cut the tarantula in half with my Japanese sword," said the principal.

Everybody was relieved. "Principal, we're glad to see you back safely," they all said.

17.

After resting for a couple of days, the principal was now able to walk with a bandage around his abdomen.

The end-of-term exams were approaching. At the morning assembly, he spoke to the students as he had always done. "Make sure to give it your all on your exams and make plans for the summer vacation so that you can have a productive break."

But looking at the way the principal walked, the students wondered whether he had been hurt.

As the students gossiped, the rumor spread; they said that the principal had fallen from a branch when he climbed up a tree to catch a beetle. The members of the Research Club kept their mouths shut and didn't let a single secret slip.

Nevertheless, many students questioned why Setsuko Minami had returned from Kansai more than a week late and why her younger sister decided to transfer to their school.

The weekly newspaper *Omoshiro-Hanbun* (Half in Jest), which Tosuke Ishikura also wrote for, issued articles about the "Biwassie Incident." On top of that, a video of Setsuko being taken away by Biwassie was going viral. There were many inquiries, and the students were having trouble answering them. Fortunately, Setsuko was back safely. But the battle against Nobunaga's troops at Kiyomizu-dera Temple was still being televised on NHK. Tosuke and the other journalists were referring to HCS Academy as the "Occult Academy" and were trying to spread this nickname.

Vice Principal Tatsue Kawaguchi addressed the students with dignity. "Many things happen in life. Let's overcome each difficulty with faith. Some media outlets report on second-generation believers in a discriminatory manner. There are also materialistic people who claim that religious groups are abusing their believers. But let's stand firm and fight against them with the spirit of self-help and the spirit of independence. On a personal level, the spirit of independence and self-reliance is essential. While knowledge is important, you need to acquire all three elements of 'wisdom,' 'love,' and 'courage' to cultivate virtue. I hope that all of you will grow to be virtuous people."

Meanwhile, Tosuke and the other atheistic journalists were still sniffing around the school. They thought they could earn more money and fame if they caused a stir. In the past, there was even a journalist who jumped on the bandwagon during a public campaign to expose the crimes of a certain cult, became a popular face on television, and eventually entered the world of politics. Tosuke and the other atheistic journalists hoped to share in similar glory as well.

One evening, Tosuke was wandering around the surrounding areas of the campus in search of an interesting story. Then, a foggy mist loomed out of the middle of Inokashira Pond. Tosuke found it strange and waited for the best opportunity to take photos with his night camera. He knew of a rumor that the Academy students might be conducting some kind of scientific experiment at the pond at night.

From out of the mist emerged a saucer-shaped UFO of about 33 feet. Tosuke was astounded and snapped many photos of it.

Soon, three cyborg-type Grey aliens, which were about four feet tall and had almond-shaped black eyes, appeared as if they were bouncing on a transparent bridge. Tosuke continued to take pictures with much excitement.

But then, the Greys spotted him.

Tosuke assumed that the alien-looking beings were kids in Halloween costumes who were just trying to scare people. He thought, *I'm only about 5'7", but I am bigger than them. I used to do judo, so it's a piece of cake for me to throw three children over my head. I'll rip off their ridiculous costumes and expose their identities.*

However, when one of the Greys in the front pointed its right middle finger toward him, his body started to float into the air. As he flailed about in the air like a butterfly swimmer, he was sucked into the small UFO. It all happened in a flash.

The UFO shot a beam into the bottom of Inokashira Pond to open up a large, manhole-like hole. The water in the pond was pushed aside as if it were being pushed back against an invisible wall. Once the UFO of about 33 feet in diameter was sucked into the bottom of the pond, the hole closed.

Underground, there was a base that was about the size of a tennis court.

Tosuke shouted, "No, this can't be happening!" But not one of the three Greys said a word.

There was a medical tent nearby. He was taken inside and laid on his back on a metal operating table; his wrists and ankles were tied up with something like leather belts. Above his head was a large light fixture for the operating table.

Two Greys in white coats were apparently scanning his entire body with a 12-inch disc that they put on like a glove on one of their hands. Tosuke's body data showed up successively on a TV-like screen.

Tosuke felt as though he heard a Grey's thought that said, "We can use this guy."

He was about to lose his mind, thinking, "Are they going to eat me like a steak?"

He heard a voice, "This man is extremely inquisitive, suspicious, and highly deceptive. He has no guilty conscience about hurting others. He fits the bill for a strike team of the flip-side universe."

Tosuke said, "Hey, what are you going to do with me? I'll write about you all as criminals. I'll call the police!"

"We don't need his body. Let's offer it to the Reptilians and have them eat it up. Let's just take out the brain and create the next Grey," said Grey A.

"Are you ogres from hell?" asked Tosuke.

"OK, give me the electric saw over there," said Grey B.

A circular electric saw of about four inches in diameter, which was attached to a metal arm, descended from the ceiling.

They injected anesthesia into Tosuke's arm. His consciousness began to fade. With a loud buzzing sound, the electric saw cut open Tosuke's skull like a lid, until his brain became exposed. A Grey with rubber gloves removed his brain using both hands and transferred it into a glass container.

Next, it brought out a Grey cyborg that was not yet in use. Tosuke's brain continued to emit a fear response. The other Greys mercilessly transplanted Tosuke's brain into the empty head of the unused Grey cyborg and connected them. Fortunately, the operation was a success.

"Let's run some current through it to check the connection," said Grey C.

For some reason, the arms and legs of Tosuke's brainless body twitched like the spinal reflex of a frog.

"Good connection," said Grey A.

"Now, we'll ask the brainwash expert to educate him and imbue his mission and awareness as an alien," said Grey D.

"As for the body, dismember it and give it to the UFO driver, Mr. Reptilian SX, for his supper," said Grey B.

And thus, Tosuke was converted into an alien cyborg.

The next day, an early-morning runner in Inokashira Park found Tosuke's camera and delivered it to the police. A series of his photographs was published in the weekly paper, *Omoshiro-Hanbun* (Half in Jest), as his last work. He was reported missing to the police.

Meanwhile, the Academy's rooftop camera had captured the entire event: the mist, the UFO, the three Greys, Tosuke taking pictures, him being taken inside the UFO with a tractor beam, and the UFO disappearing into the bottom of the pond.

Seeing what was in their photographs, the UMA Research Club members knew that Tosuke had been abducted by a UFO.

Sadly, however, there was nobody who worried about him. Dozens of people go missing every year, and he simply became one of them.

Perhaps it was a blessing for him to still be alive even just as a brain.

18.

Today is the end of the first semester—April to July. The closing ceremony was held in the gymnasium. The head of the Sun Church, Grand Master Yuho Oyama, also came to attend the ceremony as a guest of honor.

Tomorrow is the start of the long-awaited summer vacation. There will be fewer students in the dormitories, except for the twelfth graders.

After the ceremony, the cheerleading club members, who had won several national championships in a row, lined up on both sides of the path with their pom-poms. Ol' man Oyama looked happy; he broke into a smile.

However, he didn't go straight home. Instead, he held a meeting with the six students of the UMA Research Club, its two supervisors, and the principal.

"I suspect they will come today," said Grand Master Oyama.

"What do you mean?" asked Principal Reiwa.

"They'll come because you all are letting your guard down."

"I'll be on high alert all day today," said Supervisor Ishiwatari.

"I'll do anything I can to help," added Supervisor Yamaoka.

"This is the beginning of Japan's crisis. The Diet members who support constitutional revision will likely cave to the media-led public opinion and declare Japan a neutral and pacifist country. The real crisis will begin soon. The world will be divided into two sides once again, and new hardships will begin. I of course want to help the people, but they are quick to forget their gratitude as soon as they are saved," Grand Master Oyama said.

"Please tell us anything we can do to prepare," said Principal Reiwa.

"Before the day is over, prepare a week's worth of water, food, drinks, clothing, and medicine. Be ready to host a soup kitchen and make sure to have extra medicine for the sick and injured. The gymnasium will probably serve as a shelter. Bring plenty of flashlights, too," Grand Master Oyama said.

"Will there be some kind of disaster?" asked Principal Reiwa.

"You could call it that."

"Should we urge the students to stay in the school?"

"Just as children used to be evacuated to rural regions during the war, send the students who are here from regional areas back home early if you can."

Everybody began to prepare for an emergency.

A dense fog appeared around dusk.

"It's about time," Grand Master Oyama said.

A fog had covered up to 330 feet above the ground. A fire broke out in several buildings and pillars of flame extended up toward the sky from the city of Kichijoji. Fire engines roared. Out of the fog appeared a Tyrannosaurus, a Triceratops, and other creatures, and they began to destroy the shopping streets.

"This is the first round of a full-fledged attack from the parallel world. What you've experienced so far was just practice," said Grand Master Oyama.

"What can we do?" asked Hideo.

"Compare your current civilization to theirs, which has taken a different path of development, and judge things correctly. Choose the right way as a human being," Grand Master Oyama responded.

It was unbelievable. The U.S. B-29 bombers from the end of World War II appeared and began bombing the city of Tokyo indiscriminately.

Because there were now more buildings made of reinforced concrete than 80 years ago, the buildings didn't burn as much as the wooden houses did back then. Even so, the collapsing buildings still created big piles of rubble.

Japan's Self-Defense Forces scrambled their aircraft anyway, but naturally, they couldn't hide their surprise when they saw the U.S. Forces bombing Tokyo. Their modern, state-of-the-art fighters easily shot down the Grumman fighter aircraft one after another. They also shot down B-29s with their modern missiles.

However, even the Self-Defense Forces personnel couldn't believe their eyes when the Pteranodon, an ancient pterosaur, appeared. *What era are we in?*

The pterosaurs carried off the people fleeing on the ground one after another.

They also tackled the passenger planes of JAL (Japan Airlines) and ANA (All Nippon Airways) and crashed them down.

Then, from a crack in the ground, a gigantic boa constrictor—as long as 130 feet—appeared and started to devour the children, one after another.

"This is one side of the law of the universe," explained Grand Master Oyama. "Pursuing individualism will only lead to the survival of the fittest. It takes a great deal of effort to create a society of friendship, co-existence, and co-prosperity. We need great thoughts, philosophy, law, and education to do so."

Oh, how unbelievable! Next came a swarm of UFOs. There was no way the Self-Defense Forces could beat them.

The UFOs focused their attacks on the huge buildings of Tokyo. They were destroying them mainly with their laser weapons.

"Where did we go wrong?" asked Reiwa.

"We did nothing wrong," replied Grand Master Oyama. "We just have to know that there is more than one parallel world. We are actually living in a multiverse, where different timelines and space exist simultaneously. So we mustn't take our world for granted. Through this incident, God is telling humans to think about those living in other worlds as well."

Once again, Japan was turning into ruins. Giant UFOs appeared around the TV stations and newspaper publishers and were attacking their buildings right in front of their eyes. The very concept of "peace" that was commonly accepted in Japan was being shaken.

"The Japanese population of 125 million will probably decline to 80 million or so. That is when people will start to accept new ideas," said Grand Master Oyama.

A battle far beyond anybody's imagination continued to rage across Tokyo.

19.

In Japan, people's "common sense" began to shake with the emergence of the UFO fleet. They never thought that the things they turned a blind eye to and things they scoffed at could suddenly become real.

Neither compulsory education nor university education taught them the truth. The media, especially media that hired many highly educated people, have also ignored the facts and the truth. For decades, people had only taken interest in what they could see in front of their eyes or touch with their own hands. The cost of this mistake was tremendous.

The Grand Savior had already descended on earth. And yet people ignored Him and, instead, thought highly of ordinary critics, writers, scholars, and journalists—who from the perspective of human history should be considered "ideological criminals."

Human souls actually originated from God and have God's Light within, so God's mind was filled with sadness when He saw people believing that they evolved from animals and placing the greatest importance on physical survival in this world.

Of course, some evil religions poison people's souls, but there are also religions that convey the teachings of the real God or Buddha. When people are unable to distinguish good teachings from wrong ones, the Teacher of human beings knows the time has come. God has both a gentle side as "the God of Mercy" and a strict side as "the God of Judgment." When humans start to believe they have the freedom to do whatever they want and abandon their responsibilities, they stop growing spiritually. What is more, when more countries become ruled by dictators who are under the control of devils, natural disasters occur more frequently, and food and water crises start. Volcanic eruptions, great earthquakes, floods, tsunamis, and mysterious plagues are all signs indicating that it is a time when all people must become obedient and sincerely reflect on themselves. At such times, a prophet who conveys God's voice or the Grand Savior will be born somewhere in the world. Divine punishment will mercilessly befall people who spread atheism by saying, "Wars occur because there are many different religions." Divine punishment will undoubtedly befall people or races who persecuted righteous religions, too. All people must become more humble.

The first wave of attacks from the other dimensional worlds destroyed all the central functions of Japan in about three days. The major countries of the world also suffered a similar experience.

Finally, two UFO mother ships appeared; they were the giant poisonous spiders that Principal Reiwa saw in the parallel world, and they had transformed themselves into UFOs. On the bottom of the dark UFOs, one had the letter "N" while the other had the letter "S." These letters were likely the initials for North Korea and South Korea, respectively. The flashing lights around the edges of the flying saucers looked like the glowing eyes of poisonous spiders.

The spiders cast a large web over Tokyo Tower, Tokyo Skytree, and also over the government offices in Kasumigaseki, entrapping the people working there.

Although North Korea and South Korea appear to regard each other as enemies, they are both filled with resentment toward Japan. They probably share a common desire to destroy the "Empire of Japan" with their own hands once and for all.

Grand Master Yuho Oyama had already figured out their intention.

"Principal Reiwa, we're going to do what we couldn't do in the cave in the parallel world," he said.

"Master, Tokyo Tower, Tokyo Skytree, Kasumigaseki, and other central functions of Japan have all been seized. The Prime Minister's Office is probably in the same situation, as well. The attack from the other day has almost completely destroyed the Metropolitan Expressway. What can we possibly do now?" asked Principal Reiwa.

"What do you think poisonous spiders dislike the most?" Grand Master Oyama responded with a question.

"A flamethrower, perhaps? They also seem to be vulnerable to typhoons," Principal Reiwa answered.

"You mean, an attack with fire, water, and wind. OK, let's give it a try," said Grand Master Oyama.

Grand Master Yuho Oyama climbed onto the roof of the Academy and opened his arms up toward the sky.

Huge lightning bolts struck the two black UFOs, followed by loud sonic booms.

This reminded Principal Reiwa of Moses from the Old Testament.

Fires were clearly starting inside the two large UFOs.

"Shall we attack them with water next?" said Oyama.

He held out his right hand up toward Tokyo Bay. To everybody's surprise, the seawater rose out of Tokyo Bay to form two water spheres 650 feet in diameter, which floated in the air.

Yumiko from the archery club poked her sister in the arm. "What's going to happen now? What's going to happen now?"

Her sister Setsuko murmured, "I think he's gonna kindly put out the fire."

The balls of seawater from Tokyo Bay floated toward the giant UFOs and stopped right above them. Then, with a heavy splash, the balls hit the two tarantula UFOs directly and smashed them into the buildings. They were completely wrecked.

"As the finishing touch, here comes the wind," Grand Master Oyama said.

He thrust his cane in front of him and spun it clockwise.

The clouds in the sky began to swirl. Suddenly, a huge typhoon with sustained winds of at least 133 miles per hour developed in the sky above Tokyo.

The two black flying saucers were blown away into the sky as they spun violently along with the debris from the destroyed buildings.

"What's going to happen to them?" asked Hideo.

"I will drop them right onto the presidential palace and other buildings in Seoul and Pyongyang from a height of about 3,300 feet," responded Grand Master Oyama.

"They will be smashed into smithereens," said Hikaru.

"What goes around comes around," said Jiro. "Maybe those tarantulas in the parallel world are representing the collective thoughts of people in those countries."

"You're starting to understand the Truth," said Grand Master Oyama.

When the typhoon subsided, the fleet of UFOs had also disappeared from the sky above Tokyo. There was no longer a fog.

Before they knew it, the carcasses of the giant, ancient creatures had also faded away. The creatures must have gone back to another world.

A moment of peace returned to Japan.

But Grand Master Oyama didn't forget to leave his message.

"This was the first attack from the parallel world. Next, we may have to fight a decisive battle against China. It will pose the risk of nuclear war on a global scale. If the world continues to be divided as it is now, we won't be able to stop it. Young ones, do your best to change the world for the better," he said.

Having fulfilled his duties for now, Grand Master Oyama was getting ready to leave.

"At that time, will you fight with us again, Master Oyama?" Hideo called out.

"I will if I am still in good health. If I have returned to heaven by then, I shall teach you that the Primordial God also governs the multiverse," replied Grand Master Oyama.

"Thank you," they all said.

THE END

Afterword

This novel can be read as a work of fiction. However, many truths are hidden behind the story.

This is a story about how a research project, which was started by some male and female students and teachers of UMA Research Club to protect their school, contributes to unraveling the secrets of the parallel world and multiverse, and how it even saves Japan and humankind from a crisis.

I wanted to give boys, girls, and young adults dreams through this thrilling and suspenseful story that has a tint of science fiction, horror, and supernatural powers.

I wrote this novel with the hope that each one of you will become a hero of tomorrow, however small in scale it may be. I want you to learn the importance of friendship and the power of helping each other. I also want you to have the courage to confront and solve the unknown instead of simply fearing it. This is my hope as the author of this book.

Did this book *shake* your views of life?

> *Ryuho Okawa*
> *Master & CEO of Happy Science Group*
> *October 10, 2022*

For a deeper understanding of
The Novel The Shaking
see other books below by Ryuho Okawa:

Rojin, Buddha's Mystical Power [New York: IRH Press, 2021]
The Unknown Stigma 1 <The Mystery> [New York: IRH Press 2022]
The Unknown Stigma 2 <The Resurrection> [New York: IRH Press, 2022]
The Unknown Stigma 3 <The Universe> [New York: IRH Press, 2022]
The Truth about Earth, the Universe, the Spirit World: Life's Q&A with El Cantare [New York: IRH Press, 2025]

ABOUT THE AUTHOR

Founder and CEO of Happy Science Group.

Ryuho Okawa was born on July 7th, 1956, in Tokushima, Japan. After graduating from the University of Tokyo with a law degree, he joined a Tokyo-based trading company. While working at its New York headquarters, he studied international finance at the Graduate Center of the City University of New York. In 1981, he attained Great Enlightenment and became aware that he is El Cantare with a mission to bring salvation to all humankind.

In 1986, he established Happy Science. It now has members in 180 countries across the world, with more than 700 branches and temples as well as 10,000 missionary houses around the world.

He has given over 3,500 lectures (of which more than 150 are in English) and published over 3,200 books (of which more than 600 are Spiritual Interview Series), and many are translated into 42 languages. Along with *The Laws of the Sun* and *The Laws of Hell*, many of the books have become best sellers or million sellers. To date, Happy Science has produced 28 movies under his supervision. He has given the original story and concept and is also the Executive Producer. He has also composed music and written lyrics of over 450 pieces.

Moreover, he is the Founder of Happy Science University and Happy Science Academy (Junior and Senior High School), Founder and President of the Happiness Realization Party, Founder and Honorary Headmaster of Happy Science Institute of Government and Management, Founder of IRH Press Co., Ltd., and the Chairperson of NEW STAR PRODUCTION Co., Ltd. and ARI Production Co., Ltd.

BOOKS BY RYUHO OKAWA

The Laws Series

The Laws of the Sun, the first publication of the Laws Series, ranked in the annual best-selling list in Japan in 1994. After that, the Laws series' titles had always been ranked in the annual best-selling list, setting socio-cultural trends in Japan and around the world. The first three Laws series are *The Laws of the Sun*, *The Golden Laws*, and *The Laws of Eternity*.

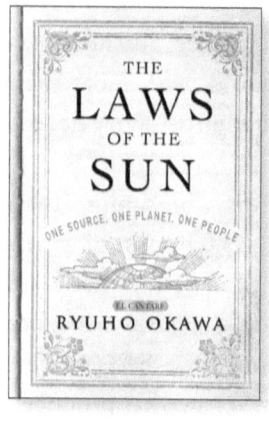

THE LAWS OF THE SUN

ONE SOURCE, ONE PLANET, ONE PEOPLE

Paperback • 288 pages • $15.95
ISBN: 978-1-942125-43-3 (Oct. 25, 2018)

IMAGINE IF YOU COULD ASK GOD why He created this world and about the spiritual laws He used to shape us and everything around us. If we could understand His designs and intentions, we could discover what our goals in life should be and whether our actions move us closer to those goals or farther away.

At a young age, a spiritual calling prompted Ryuho Okawa to outline what he innately understood to be universal truths for all humankind. In *The Laws of the Sun*, Okawa outlines these laws of the universe and provides a road map for living one's life with greater purpose and meaning. In this powerful book, Ryuho Okawa reveals the transcendent nature of consciousness and the secrets of the multidimensional universe as well as the meaning of humans that exist within it. By understanding the different stages of love and following the Buddhist Eightfold Path, he believes we can speed up our eternal process of development. *The Laws of the Sun* shows the way to realize true happiness—a happiness that continues from this world through the other.

THE LAWS OF ETERNITY
EL CANTARE UNVEILS THE STRUCTURE OF THE SPIRIT WORLD

Paperback • 224 pages • $17.95
ISBN: 978-1-958655-16-0 (May 15, 2024)

"Where do we come from and where do we go after death?"

This unparalleled book offers us complete answers to life's most important questions that we all are confronted with at some point or another. In *The Laws of Eternity*, author Ryuho Okawa takes us on a journey to the other world, a place where we came from before we were born and return to after death.

This book reveals the eternal mysteries and the ultimate secrets of Earth's spirit group that have been covered by the veil of legends and myths. Encountering the long-hidden Eternal Truths that are revealed for the first time in human history will change the way you live your life now.

Unlocking the Secret of the Universe

THE TRUTH ABOUT EARTH, THE UNIVERSE, THE SPIRIT WORLD

LIFE'S Q&A WITH EL CANTARE

Paperback • 180 pages • $17.95
ISBN: 978-1-958655-26-9 (Jun. 17, 2025)

While the non-existence of the spirit or the Spirit World has never been definitively proven, Okawa provides profound yet clear answers to each unique spiritual question without a script. His insights reveal that he is no ordinary spiritual leader, but a figure of immense wisdom and enlightenment—a living Buddha—possessing a comprehensive understanding of the vast, multidimensional nature of the universe and the very essence of existence.

The Truth about the Spirit World

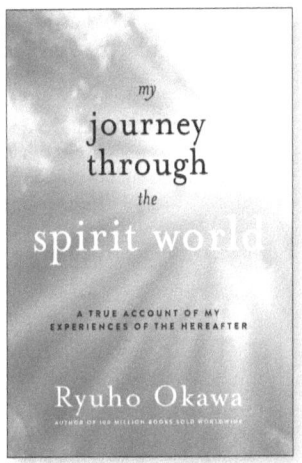

MY JOURNEY THROUGH THE SPIRIT WORLD
A TRUE ACCOUNT OF MY EXPERIENCES OF THE HEREAFTER

Paperback • 224 pages • $15.95
ISBN: 978-1-942125-41-9 (Jul. 25, 2018)

What happens when we die? What is the afterworld like? Do heaven and hell really exist? In this book, Ryuho Okawa shares surprising facts such as that we visit the spirit world during sleep, that souls in the spirit world go to a school to learn about how to use their spiritual power, and that people continue to live in the same lifestyle as they did in this world. This unique and authentic guide to the spirit world will awaken us to the truth of life and death, and show us how we should start living so that we can return to a bright world of heaven.

Novel Series

THE UNKNOWN STIGMA 1
<THE MYSTERY>

Hardcover • 192 pages • $17.95
ISBN: 978-1-942125-28-0 (Oct. 1, 2022)

The first spiritual mystery novel by Ryuho Okawa. It happened one early summer afternoon, in a densely wooded park in Tokyo: following a loud scream of a young woman, the alleged victim was found lying with his eyes rolled back and foaming at the mouth. But there was no sign of forced trauma, nor even a drop of blood. Then, similar murder cases continued one after another without any clues. Later, this mysterious serial murder case leads back to a young Catholic nun...

THE UNKNOWN STIGMA 2
<THE RESURRECTION>

Hardcover • 180 pages • $17.95
ISBN: 978-1-942125-31-0 (Nov. 1, 2022)

A sequel to *The Unknown Stigma 1 <The Mystery>* by Ryuho Okawa. After an extraordinary spiritual experience, a young, mysterious Catholic nun is now endowed with a new, noble mission. What kind of destiny will she face? Will it be hope or despair that awaits her? The story develops into a turn of events that no one could ever have anticipated. Are you ready to embrace its shocking ending?

THE UNKNOWN STIGMA 3
<THE UNIVERSE>

Hardcover • 184 pages • $17.95
ISBN: 978-1-958655-00-9 (Dec. 1, 2022)

In this astonishing sequel to the first two installments of *The Unknown Stigma*, the protagonist journeys through the universe and encounters a mystical world unknown to humankind. Discover what awaits her beyond this mysterious world.

Recommended Books

ROJIN, BUDDHA'S MYSTICAL POWER
ITS ULTIMATE ATTAINMENT IN TODAY'S WORLD
Paperback • 224 pages • $16.95
ISBN: 978-1-942125-82-2 (Sep. 24, 2021)

In this book, Ryuho Okawa has redefined the traditional Buddhist term *Rojin* and explained that in modern society it means the following: the ability for individuals with great spiritual powers to live in the world as people with common sense while using their abilities to the optimal level. This book will unravel the mystery of the mind and lead you to the path to enlightenment.

SPIRITUAL MESSAGES FROM YAIDRON SAVE THE WORLD FROM DESTRUCTION
Paperback • $11.95 • ISBN: 978-1-943928-23-1
E-book • $10.99 • ISBN: 978-1-943928-25-5

In this book, Yaidron explains what was going on behind the military coup in Myanmar and Taliban's control over Afghanistan. He also warns of the imminent danger approaching Taiwan. What is now going on is a battle between democratic values and the communist one-party control. How to overcome this battle and create peace on Earth depends on the faith and righteous actions of each one of us.

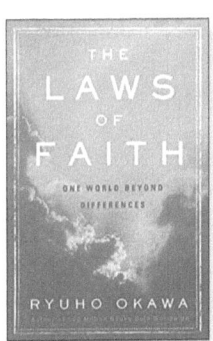

THE LAWS OF FAITH
ONE WORLD BEYOND DIFFERENCES
Paperback • 208 pages • $15.95
ISBN: 978-1-942125-34-1 (Mar. 31, 2018)

In this book, Ryuho Okawa preaches the core teachings of the world religion and the faith in the God of Earth. By integrating logical and spiritual viewpoints, Okawa gives answers to modern-day problems that traditional religions cannot solve. Through this book, you will learn to go beyond different values, harmonize with each other and between nations, and create a world filled with peace and prosperity.

The Latest Titles

ONE MORE STEP FORWARD
THE INVINCIBLE THINKING TO GET YOU THROUGH TOUGH TIMES

Paperback • 256 pages • $17.95
ISBN: 978-1-958655-25-2 (May 7, 2025)

Ryuho Okawa is a true self-made man with an indomitable spirit to bring happiness to all humankind. His drive to keep moving forward by taking steady steps through the power of discipline has led to the publication of over 3,200 books in just 37 years. Unlock the keys to lifelong growth and success by reading this book.

THE WAY TO HUMAN PERFECTION
BEST SELECTION OF RYUHO OKAWA'S EARLY LECTURES (VOLUME 2)

Paperback • 200 pages • $17.95
ISBN: 978-1-958655-20-7 (Oct. 22, 2024)

The path to enlightenment starts from understanding 'the eternal viewpoint of life.' Through each chapter, Ryuho Okawa navigates us to shift the perspective of ourselves from a 'finite self' living a limited life to an 'eternal self' living an eternal life.

THE ETERNAL BUDDHA
NOW, HERE, IS THE IMPERISHABLE LIGHT

Hardcover • 200 pages • $17.95
ISBN: 978-1-958655-19-1 (Sep 15, 2024)

This book is a powerful source of guidance for those seeking Truth. Embedded within, you will find the infinite wisdom of the Eternal Buddha and come to realize that you are not just a physical being, but an eternal soul of brilliant light. Through the words of the Eternal Buddha, unlock the boundless treasures of enlightenment given to humankind in this modern era.

Buddhist Teachings for People Today

THE ESSENCE OF BUDDHA
THE PATH TO ENLIGHTENMENT
Paperback • 208 pages • $14.95
ISBN: 978-1-942125-06-8 (Oct. 1, 2016)

The essence of Shakyamuni Buddha's original teachings of the mind are explained in simple words. Through this book, you will learn how to attain inner happiness, the wisdom to conquer ego, and to enter the path to enlightenment. It is a way of life that people in this modern age can practice to achieve lifelong self-growth.

THE CHALLENGE OF ENLIGHTENMENT
NOW, HERE, THE NEW DHARMA WHEEL TURNS
Paperback • 380 pages • $17.95
ISBN: 978-1-942125-92-1 (Dec. 20, 2022)

Buddha's teachings, a reflection of his eternal wisdom, are like a bamboo pole used to change the course of your boat in the rapid stream of the great river called life. By reading this book, your mind becomes clearer and learns to savor inner peace, and you will be empowered to make profound life improvements.

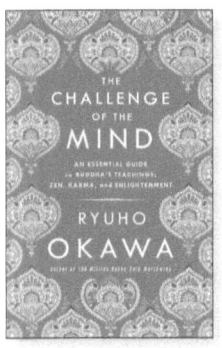

THE CHALLENGE OF THE MIND
AN ESSENTIAL GUIDE TO BUDDHA'S TEACHINGS: ZEN, KARMA AND ENLIGHTENMENT
Paperback • 208 pages • $16.95
ISBN: 978-1-942125-45-7 (Nov. 15, 2018)

In this book, Ryuho Okawa explains essential Buddhist tenets and how to put them into practice. Enlightenment is not just an abstract idea but one that everyone can experience to some extent. Okawa offers a solid basis of reason and an intellectual understanding of Buddhist concepts.

WHO IS EL CANTARE?

El Cantare means "the Light of the Earth." He is the Supreme God of the Earth who has been guiding humankind since the beginning of Genesis, and He is the Creator of the universe. He is whom Jesus called Father and Muhammad called Allah and is *Ame-no-Mioya-Gami*, Japanese Father God. Different parts of El Cantare's core consciousness have descended to Earth in the past, once as Alpha and another as Elohim. His branch spirits, such as Shakyamuni Buddha and Hermes, have descended to Earth many times and helped to flourish many civilizations. To unite various religions and to integrate various fields of study in order to build a new civilization on Earth, a part of the core consciousness has descended to Earth as Master Ryuho Okawa.

Alpha is a part of the core consciousness of El Cantare who descended to Earth around 330 million years ago. Alpha preached Earth's Truths to harmonize and unify Earth-born humans and space people who came from other planets.

Elohim is a part of the core consciousness of El Cantare who descended to Earth around 150 million years ago. He gave wisdom, mainly on the differences between light and darkness, good and evil.

Ame-no-Mioya-Gami (Japanese Father God) is the Creator God and the Father God who appears in ancient literature, *Hotsuma Tsutae*. It is believed that He descended on the foothills of Mt. Fuji about 30,000 years ago and built the Fuji dynasty, which is the root of the Japanese civilization. With justice as the central pillar, Ame-no-Mioya-Gami's teachings spread to ancient civilizations of other countries in the world.

Shakyamuni Buddha was born in Lumbini (now located in Nepal) around 2,600 years ago as the prince of the Shakya clan. When he was 29 years old, he renounced the world and sought enlightenment. He later attained Great Enlightenment in Bodh Gaya, India and founded Buddhism, which has spread extensively throughout Asia.

Hermes is one of the 12 Olympian gods in Greek mythology, but the spiritual Truth is that he taught the teachings of love and progress around 4,300 years ago which became the origin of the current Western civilization. He is a hero who truly existed.

Ophealis was born in Greece around 6,500 years ago and was the leader who took an expedition to as far as Egypt. He is the God of miracles, prosperity, and arts, and is known as Osiris in Egyptian mythology.

Rient Arl Croud was born as a king of the ancient Incan Empire around 7,000 years ago and taught about the mysteries of the mind. In the heavenly world, he is responsible for the interactions that take place between various planets.

Thoth was an almighty leader who built the golden age of the Atlantic civilization around 12,000 years ago. In Egyptian mythology, he is known as God Thoth.

Ra Mu was a leader who built the golden age of the civilization of Mu around 17,000 years ago. As a religious leader and a politician, he ruled by uniting religion and politics.

ABOUT HAPPY SCIENCE

Happy Science is a religious group founded on the faith in El Cantare who is the God of the Earth, and the Creator of the universe. The essence of human beings is the soul that was created by God, and we all are children of God. God is our true parent, so in our souls, we have a fundamental desire to "believe in God, love God, and get closer to God." And, we can get closer to God by living with God's Will as our own. In Happy Science, we call this the "Exploration of Right Mind." More specifically, it means to practice the Fourfold Path, which consists of "Love, Wisdom, Self-Reflection, and Progress."

Love: Love means "love that gives," or mercy. God hopes for the happiness of all people. Therefore, living with God's Will as our own means to start by practicing "love that gives."

Wisdom: God's love is boundless. It is important to learn various Truths in order to understand the heart of God.

Self-Reflection: Once you learn the heart of God and the difference between His mind and yours, you should strive to bring your own mind closer to the mind of God—that process is called self-reflection. Self-reflection also includes meditation and prayer.

Progress: Since God hopes for the happiness of all people, you should also make progress in your love, and make an effort to realize utopia in which everyone in your society, country, and eventually all humankind can become happy.

As we practice this Fourfold Path, our souls will advance toward God step by step. That is when we can attain real happiness—our souls' desire to get closer to God comes true.

In Happy Science, we conduct activities to make ourselves happy through belief in Lord El Cantare and to spread this faith to the world and bring happiness to all. We welcome you to join our activities!

We hold events and activities to help you practice the Fourfold Path at our branches, temples, missionary centers, and missionary houses

Love: We hold various volunteering activities. Our members conduct missionary work together as the greatest practice of love.

Wisdom: We offer our comprehensive collection of books of Truth, many of which are available online and at Happy Science locations. In addition, we offer numerous opportunities such as seminars or book clubs to learn the Truth.

Self-Reflection: We offer opportunities to polish your mind through self-reflection, meditation, and prayer. Many members have experienced improvement in their human relationships by changing their own minds.

Progress: We also offer seminars to enhance your power of influence. Because it is also important to do well at work to make society better, we hold seminars to improve your work and management skills.

HAPPY SCIENCE'S ENGLISH SUTRA

"The True Words Spoken By Buddha"

"The True Words Spoken By Buddha" is an English sutra given directly from the spirit of Shakyamuni Buddha, who is a part of Master Ryuho Okawa's subconscious. The words in this sutra are not of a mere human being but are the words of God or Buddha sent directly from the ninth dimension, which is the highest realm of the Earth's Spirit World.

"The True Words Spoken By Buddha" is an essential sutra for us to connect and live with God or Buddha's Will as our own.

MEMBERSHIPS

MEMBERSHIP

If you would like to know more about Happy Science, please consider becoming a member. Those who pledge to believe in Lord El Cantare and wish to learn more can join us.

When you become a member, you will receive the following sutras: "The True Words Spoken By Buddha," "Prayer to the Lord" and "Prayer to Guardian and Guiding Spirits."

DEVOTEE MEMBER

If you would like to learn the teachings of Happy Science and walk the path of faith, become a Devotee member who pledges devotion to the Three Treasures, which are Buddha, Dharma, and Sangha. Buddha refers to Lord El Cantare, Master Ryuho Okawa. Dharma refers to Master Ryuho Okawa's teachings. Sangha refers to Happy Science. Devoting to the Three Treasures will let your Buddha nature shine, and you will enter the path to attain true freedom of the mind.

Becoming a devotee means you become Buddha's disciple. You will discipline your mind and act to bring happiness to society.

✉ EMAIL or ☎ PHONE CALL
Please turn to the contact information page.

🔗 ONLINE [member.happy-science.org/signup/]

CONTACT INFORMATION

Happy Science is a worldwide organization with branches and temples around the globe. For full details, visit happy-science.org. The following are some of our main Happy Science locations:

UNITED STATES AND CANADA

New York
79 Franklin St., New York, NY 10013, USA
Phone: 1-212-343-7972
Fax: 1-212-343-7973
Email: ny@happy-science.org
Website: happyscience-usa.org

New Jersey
66 Hudson St., #2R, Hoboken, NJ 07030, USA
Phone: 1-201-313-0127
Email: nj@happy-science.org
Website: happyscience-usa.org

Chicago
33 West Higgins Rd. 4040,
South Barrington, IL 60010, USA
Phone: 1-630-937-3077
Email: chicago@happy-science.org
Website: happyscience-usa.org

Florida
5208 8th St., Zephyrhills, FL 33542, USA
Phone: 1-813-715-0000
Fax: 1-813-715-0010
Email: florida@happy-science.org
Website: happyscience-usa.org

Atlanta
1874 Piedmont Ave., NE Suite 360-C
Atlanta, GA 30324, USA
Phone: 1-404-892-7770
Email: atlanta@happy-science.org
Website: happyscience-usa.org

San Francisco
525 Clinton St.
Redwood City, CA 94062, USA
Phone & Fax: 1-650-363-2777
Email: sf@happy-science.org
Website: happyscience-usa.org

Los Angeles
1590 E. Del Mar Blvd., Pasadena,
CA 91106, USA
Phone: 1-626-395-7775
Fax: 1-626-395-7776
Email: la@happy-science.org
Website: happyscience-usa.org

Orange County
16541 Gothard St. Suite 104
Huntington Beach, CA 92647
Phone: 1-714-659-1501
Email: oc@happy-science.org
Website: happyscience-usa.org

San Diego
7841 Balboa Ave. Suite #202
San Diego, CA 92111, USA
Phone: 1-626-395-7775
Fax: 1-626-395-7776
E-mail: sandiego@happy-science.org
Website: happyscience-usa.org

Hawaii
Phone: 1-808-591-9772
Fax: 1-808-591-9776
Email: hi@happy-science.org
Website: happyscience-usa.org

Kauai
3343 Kanakolu Street, Suite 5
Lihue, HI 96766, USA
Phone: 1-808-822-7007
Fax: 1-808-822-6007
Email: kauai-hi@happy-science.org
Website: happyscience-usa.org

Toronto
845 The Queensway
Etobicoke, ON M8Z 1N6, Canada
Phone: 1-416-901-3747
Email: toronto@happy-science.org
Website: happy-science.ca

Vancouver
#201-2607 East 49th Avenue,
Vancouver, BC, V5S 1J9, Canada
Phone: 1-604-437-7735
Fax: 1-604-437-7764
Email: vancouver@happy-science.org
Website: happy-science.ca

INTERNATIONAL

Tokyo
1-6-7 Togoshi, Shinagawa,
Tokyo, 142-0041, Japan
Phone: 81-3-6384-5770
Fax: 81-3-6384-5776
Email: tokyo@happy-science.org
Website: happy-science.org

London
3 Margaret St.
London, W1W 8RE United Kingdom
Phone: 44-20-7323-9255
Fax: 44-20-7323-9344
Email: eu@happy-science.org
Website: www.happyscience-uk.org

Sydney
516 Pacific Highway, Lane Cove North,
2066 NSW, Australia
Phone: 61-2-9411-2877
Fax: 61-2-9411-2822
Email: sydney@happy-science.org

Sao Paulo
Rua. Domingos de Morais 1154,
Vila Mariana, Sao Paulo SP
CEP 04010-100, Brazil
Phone: 55-11-5088-3800
Email: sp@happy-science.org
Website: happyscience.com.br

Jundiai
Rua Congo, 447, Jd. Bonfiglioli
Jundiai-CEP, 13207-340, Brazil
Phone: 55-11-4587-5952
Email: jundiai@happy-science.org

Seoul
74, Sadang-ro 27-gil,
Dongjak-gu, Seoul, Korea
Phone: 82-2-3478-8777
Fax: 82-2-3478-9777
Email: korea@happy-science.org

Taipei
No. 89, Lane 155, Dunhua N. Road,
Songshan District, Taipei City 105, Taiwan
Phone: 886-2-2719-9377
Fax: 886-2-2719-5570
Email: taiwan@happy-science.org

Taichung
No. 146, Minzu Rd., Central Dist.,
Taichung City 400001, Taiwan
Phone: 886-4-22233777
Email: taichung@happy-science.org

Kuala Lumpur
No 22A, Block 2, Jalil Link Jalan Jalil Jaya 2, Bukit Jalil 57000,
Kuala Lumpur, Malaysia
Phone: 60-3-8998-7877
Fax: 60-3-8998-7977
Email: malaysia@happy-science.org
Website: happyscience.org.my

Kathmandu
Kathmandu Metropolitan City,
Ward No. 15, Ring Road, Kimdol,
Sitapaila Kathmandu, Nepal
Phone: 977-1-537-2931
Email: nepal@happy-science.org

Kampala
Plot 877 Rubaga Road, Kampala
P.O. Box 34130 Kampala, Uganda
Email: uganda@happy-science.org

ABOUT HS PRESS

HS Press is an imprint of IRH Press Co., Ltd. IRH Press Co., Ltd., based in Tokyo, was founded in 1987 as a publishing division of Happy Science. IRH Press publishes religious and spiritual books, journals, and magazines and also operates broadcast and film production enterprises. For more information, visit *okawabooks.com*.

Follow us on:

- Facebook: Okawa Books
- Youtube: Okawa Books
- Pinterest: Okawa Books
- Instagram: OkawaBooks
- Twitter: Okawa Books
- Goodreads: Ryuho Okawa

---- NEWSLETTER ----

To receive book-related news, promotions, and events, please subscribe to our newsletter below.

okawabooks.com/pages/subscribe

AUDIO / VISUAL MEDIA

YOUTUBE   PODCAST

Visit the above to learn more about Ryuho Okawa's books. Topics range from self-help, current affairs, spirituality, religion, and the universe.

www.ingramcontent.com/pod-product-compliance
Lightning Source LLC
LaVergne TN
LVHW091048100526
838202LV00077B/3321